Apr. 30, 2010

MISSING
IN
ACTION

Also by Dean Hughes
Search and Destroy
Soldier Boys

MISSING
IN
ACTION

J
HUG

DEAN HUGHES

ATHENEUM BOOKS FOR YOUNG READERS
NEW YORK LONDON TORONTO SYDNEY

ATHENEUM BOOKS FOR YOUNG READERS
An imprint of Simon & Schuster Children's Publishing Division
1230 Avenue of the Americas, New York, New York 10020
ATHENEUM BOOKS FOR YOUNG READERS is a registered trademark of
Simon & Schuster, Inc.
For information about special discounts for bulk purchases,
please contact Simon & Schuster Special Sales at 1-866-506-1949
or business@simonandschuster.com.
The Simon & Schuster Speakers Bureau can bring authors to your
live event. For more information or to book an event, contact the
Simon & Schuster Speakers Bureau at 1-866-248-3049 or visit our
website at www.simonspeakers.com.
The text for this book is set in Garth Graphic.
Manufactured in the United States of America
0110 MTN
First Edition
10 9 8 7 6 5 4 3 2 1
Library of Congress Cataloging-in-Publication Data
Hughes, Dean, 1943–
Missing in action / Dean Hughes. — 1st ed.
p. cm.
Summary: While his father is missing in action in the Pacific
during World War II, twelve-year-old Jay moves with his mother
to small-town Utah, where he sees prejudice from both sides, as
a part-Navajo himself and through an unlikely friendship with
Japanese American Ken from the nearby internment camp.
ISBN 978-1-4169-1502-7 (hardcover)
[1. Prejudices—Fiction. 2. Japanese Americans—Evacuation and
relocation, 1942–1945—Fiction. 3. Racially mixed people—Fiction.
4. Baseball—Fiction. 5. Grandparents—Fiction. 6. World War,
1939–1945—Fiction. 7. Family life—Utah—Fiction. 8. Utah—
History—20th century—Fiction.] I. Title.
PZ7.H87312Mis 2010
[Fic]—dc22
2009011276

For my grandson, David Russell

ACKNOWLEDGMENTS

Thanks to Fred C. Adams, who lived in Delta, Utah, during World War II and was willing to take time with me to share his memories; and to Jane Beckwith, expert on the history of the Topaz Relocation Center and president of the Topaz Museum Board, who took a day out of her busy life to answer my long list of questions.

MISSING
IN
ACTION

CHAPTER 1

JAY THACKER WAS STANDING BY THE BACKSTOP. HIS BASEBALL GLOVE was tucked under his arm. For now, he was just watching. He was new in town and he didn't know any of the boys who were out on the field. Most of them weren't very good players—he could see that— but then, he wasn't that great himself. He thought he'd like to play, but he didn't want to say so.

The boys were playing workup, not teams, and one guy—Gordy, everyone kept calling him—had stayed up to bat three or four times. He was standing at first base now, chattering on and on, trying to bother the pitcher. His voice sounded rough, like the sound a shovel makes, hitting into gravel. "You better watch me, Freddy," he kept saying. "I'm taking off. I'm gonna steal second." And then, after Freddy bounced a pitch in the dirt, "You throw like my grandma. You can't pitch."

Jay couldn't help smiling. This Gordy kid really thought he was good.

Gordy turned and looked toward the outfield. "Move back, boys. Lew's going to hit the ball over your heads. He's gonna bring me home."

Lew was big, but he swung at the next pitch and knocked a little blooper out into shallow left field. Gordy ran hard to second and then kept right on going for third. The boy in left ran in for the ball and fielded it okay. He should've thrown Gordy out, easy, but he tried to hurry and tossed the ball clear over the third baseman's head. The ball rolled out into the street and Gordy ran on home. He jumped on the plate with both feet, then spun around and yelled, "You're never going to get us out. We're the Bronx Bombers." Then his head jerked around and he said, "Hey, kid, do you want to play?"

It took Jay a second or two to realize Gordy meant him. "I guess so," he said.

"Head out to right field. That'll give 'em four outfielders, but it won't make no difference. Those guys are sorry excuses for ballplayers. You any good?"

"Not really. I—"

"Who are you anyway?"

By then he was walking around the backstop, which was nothing more than chicken wire nailed onto some pine poles. "My name's Jay Thacker."

2

"Where'd you come from?"

"Salt Lake City."

"Uh-oh." Gordy turned toward the field again. "Hey, we got us a big-city boy here. Maybe he can play. You better hope so. You sad sacks need all the help you can get." He looked back at Jay and grinned.

Gordy was wearing a faded red baseball cap. Whitish hair, stiff as straw, was sticking out from under it. His face was sunburned and skin was peeling off his nose and ears. His top teeth were goofy, like they were too big for his mouth. At least he'd noticed Jay and asked him to play.

He trotted out to right field and waited to see what might happen, but he was glad when the first few batters didn't hit the ball his way. He didn't want to make an error right off and have to listen to Gordy say something about that.

One kid hit a grounder to first base and made an out. That meant Freddy, the guy who'd been pitching, finally made it up to bat. He struck out his first time up, though. He couldn't hit any better than he could pitch. At least Jay knew he was better than that guy. Gordy and Lew both kept getting on base, but half the time it was because of errors. That didn't stop Gordy from telling everyone how great he was.

Jay worked his way around to left field, and then he made a decent play on a grounder that bounced past the shortstop. He threw to second and his toss was a little off line, but he didn't end up looking too bad. Gordy yelled at him, "Hey, Thacker, you're the best one out there. You didn't fall on your face—and I figured you might."

Jay didn't say anything. Some of the guys were yelling at Gordy, telling him he wasn't as hot as he thought he was. But Jay had never been able to do anything like that.

After a while Lew hit a fly ball that was caught by a short kid out in center. The kid ran toward home plate and Lew ran out to center. That meant they were playing "flies go up." Right after that another guy struck out, so Jay moved over to third base and Gordy was up for about the eighth or ninth time. "Look out, boys," he yelled. "This time I'm going for the fence. You better move *way* back."

The sun was getting low in the sky now, but the air was still hot. Sweat was running off Jay's face. He used his shirt to wipe his eyes.

Gordy took a big swing at the first pitch and slammed a hard grounder straight at Jay. He was ready, but the ball skipped over his glove and hit him like a fist, right in the throat. He dropped to his knees and grabbed his neck. He was choking, but he didn't want to look stupid, so he stood up as quick as he could. Tears were running down his cheeks, not from crying, but just from coughing and trying to swallow.

Gordy came running out. "Hey, you all right?"

"Sure," he tried to say.

"Did it hit your chin or . . . oh man, it caught you right in the throat, didn't it?"

"I'm okay." Some of the other guys were coming over.

"Can you swallow all right?"

"Yeah." And he could now. But it hurt.

"Hey, I gotta tell ya, man. You're tough as nails. That was a *blue darter* I hit at you." Gordy grinned, showing those funny teeth again. "That woulda put a lot of guys flat on their back."

He was thinking he didn't want to stick around and play anymore. He didn't want to say that, though, not with Gordy talking that way about him.

"Are you a Indian?"

"What?"

"You look like a Indian."

He wasn't sure what to say. He didn't like to talk about that. "My dad's half Navajo." More guys were gathering around him now. Lew had come in from left field.

"No wonder you can take a blow and get back up," Gordy said. "You got Indian blood in you."

He didn't mind that, but he knew all the bad things people said about Indians. He'd heard plenty of that in Salt Lake. Indians were dirty and lazy—stuff like that. He didn't want these guys to think that's what he was.

"What are you doing in Delta?"

He was getting his breath back now, and his throat didn't feel all stopped up. He wanted the game to get going again. "Me and my mom came down here to live for a while. My dad's in the war." But talking made him cough again.

Gordy gave him a couple of slaps on the back, like that was going to help out somehow. "Where's he fighting?"

"Out in the Pacific. He's in the navy." He didn't want to tell the rest.

"Whereabouts?"

He rubbed his hand over his throat, and then he flicked away some tears from one cheek. "We don't know exactly."

"Yeah. It's prob'ly secret. I know what you're talking about. What's he on? A battleship?"

Jay tried to think of something else to say, but he couldn't think of anything. So he said it. "His ship went down. He's missing in action."

Jay saw Gordy's reaction, the way his head jerked back. All the boys had been holding their gloves under their arms, kind of waiting, like they wished Gordy wouldn't carry this on so long. Now they were changed. They were staring at Jay, and he knew what they were thinking.

Gordy said it out loud. "My dad says 'missing in action' just about always turns into 'killed in action.'"

"My dad's not dead, though," he said, louder than he meant to say it. "He's a good swimmer. He probably made it to an island or something like that. Or he could've been picked up by the Japs and made into a prisoner of war."

"Hey, that's worse than death," Gordy said. "The Japs starve people and torture 'em. They pull out their fingernails with pliers—all that kind of stuff."

"Come on, Gordy," one of the boys said. "He probably made it to an island. You don't need to—"

"Hey look, Eldred, I'm not saying he's dead. Or that the Japs are working him over. I'm just saying that's how it is when they get hold of you. Everybody knows that."

"My dad's alive," Jay said. "When the war's over, he'll come home."

"I think he'll probably get home," Gordy said. "I'll bet he's as tough as you—maybe tougher. He's half Indian, not just a quarter."

At least he hadn't said Jay's dad was lazy or dirty.

"Lay off, Gordy," Eldred said. "You don't need to get into all that." Eldred was the short kid who had caught the ball out in center. He wore wire eyeglasses that made his eyes look big.

"How long's he been missing?" asked Gordy.

"I can't remember exactly."

But he did remember. His dad had joined the navy right after the war broke out, and his ship had been sunk early in the year—February 1943—out by the Solomon Islands. He'd looked at a map; he knew where they were, clear down by Australia. That had been four months ago—a little more than that. If Jay told Gordy, though, he would say that was a long time not to hear.

Gordy only nodded—like maybe he knew Jay didn't want to talk about it anymore. He even said, "So do you guys want to keep trying to get me out, or have you had enough for one night?"

The sun was glowing, turning orange, and Jay knew it had to be pretty late. In June, here in the desert, the sun never seemed to go down, especially on "war time"—with all the clocks set forward.

"I gotta go," a little kid said—a guy who had made more errors than anyone.

"You're no big loss, Will," Gordy told him.

But some of the other guys said they had to get home too, and the game broke up. Jay took a step away, but Gordy said, "Where you living, Chief?"

He stopped and looked back, surprised by the name.

"His name's not Chief," Eldred said.

"It is now. That's what I'm going to call him. You don't care, do you, Chief?"

"My name's Jay."

"I know. But I like that name. Chief. It fits you. 'Cause you're tough and everything."

He didn't want to be called that, but he didn't say so.

"So where you living?"

"With my Grandpa Reid."

"Kimball Reid? From the drugstore?"

"Yeah."

"He's your grandpa?" Gordy looked surprised. "I didn't know one of his kids married a Indian."

Lew had stepped over next to Gordy. "No kidding. Brother Reid's your grandpa?"

He nodded.

"He gave me my patriarchal blessing."

Jay knew his grandpa was the patriarch in Delta. That was something in the church—the Mormon church—but he wasn't exactly sure what it meant.

"Before he was patriarch, he was my bishop," Eldred said. "He's about the best man in this whole valley. I've heard my dad say that."

He could see that all three of the boys were looking at him in a new way. Eldred's big eyes were staring hard at him. Jay said, "I'll tell you what else. My dad's a war hero. Before his ship got sunk, he won some medals. Quite a few."

"Which ones?" asked Gordy.

"I can't remember what they're called."

"A silver star or a bronze? Anything like that?"

"Yeah. I think so."

"Hey, then, he *is* tough. He can stand up to the Japs, all right. He's not a drunk, is he?"

"What?"

"A lot of Navajos are drunks. And they'll steal anything that ain't tied down. My dad don't trust any of 'em."

"My dad doesn't steal," he said, loud again.

"I didn't say he did. That's just my dad talking. I know some other stuff. Indians can run fast—a lot of 'em. And they know everything about hunting and tracking down animals, all those things. Is that how you are?"

He didn't think so. But he didn't say that. He said, "I can run pretty fast."

"You can take a hard grounder in the throat, too, and get back up."

Eldred shook his head. "Don't start that again, Gordy." Eldred's overalls were all faded out and too small for him. He had his hat off now, and Jay could see that his hair was cut straight around, like maybe his mom had cut it, not a barber.

"So are you going to live here for the rest of the war?" Lew asked. He was taller than any of the kids. He had a nose that looked flattened out a little, like it had gotten broken sometime. He looked mean, a little, but he didn't sound that way. He'd gotten a lot of hits, the same as Gordy, and he hadn't yelled about it.

"I don't know how long we'll stay," he said. He touched his hand to his Adam's apple. He could feel that the skin had been roughed up, but the pain was deeper in, like a bruise.

"We play ball pretty much every night once the sun drops down a little," said Lew. "It gets too hot in the day—and most of us have to work around our own places in the mornings. But you can come over any night you want to and just about always get in a game."

"How old are you, Jay?" Eldred asked.

"Almost thirteen."

"Is that right? I figured you for fourteen. Most of us will be in eighth grade next year, some in seventh. The high school boys play on the good diamond—the one the town team plays on—so we come over here. That way, nobody bothers us."

"Do you have any arrowheads, Chief?" Gordy asked, like that was what everyone had been talking about. His hands were stuck into the front pockets of his jeans—old ones that had been patched in the knees a couple of times. He had a grass stain across the shoulder of the old undershirt he was wearing. He was still grinning. Jay didn't know why.

"Grandpa has some arrowheads, but I don't," he said.

"You ain't much of a Indian, are you?" Gordy laughed, making a scratchy sound, like the way he talked. "Around here, we collect arrowheads. I've got about two dozen, I guess, if you count broke pieces. We go out in the desert and look for 'em, or we go over by Topaz Mountain and look for chunks of topaz, and we shoot BB guns. You ever done stuff like that?"

"No."

"Do you want to?"

"I guess."

"We'll have to teach you the stuff a Indian is supposed to know."

"I'm not an Indian. I'm just—"

"I know all that. But we'll teach you about the desert—and how to find stuff out there. When we can get ammo for our .22 rifles, we shoot rabbits. Or we just shoot what we can with our BB guns. We'll show you all that stuff."

Jay was nodding again, but he wasn't sure about any of this. Everything was different here. Maybe he and his mom should have stayed in Salt Lake. He didn't want everyone, right off, thinking he was an Indian.

CHAPTER 2

THE BOYS WALKED OVER TO MAIN STREET TOGETHER. GORDY KEPT talking the whole time—asking him about Salt Lake City, the Great Salt Lake, all kinds of things. And then, when they reached Second West, the street with the nicest houses, Jay said good-bye. His grandma and grandpa had a house on that street. It was old but big—a lot bigger than any place he'd lived in before. That was okay, but sometimes Grandpa tried to act like he was his dad, not telling him what to do, but asking him all about everything.

Everything here was different. He didn't like it much so far. Grandma was nice, but he'd heard her talking to Mom about his dad, saying things that weren't exactly right. His dad was a good ballplayer. And he was funny, always making jokes and everything. Grandma didn't know about things like that. She didn't have to be saying things about him.

When he got back to the house, his mom was sitting out on the porch. "Jay, you promised me you'd be home by nine o'clock," she said. She sounded upset. That's how she was a lot lately.

He stepped up onto the porch. "What time is it?" he asked.

His mom was wearing slacks—something Grandpa didn't like very much—and her hair was loose, hanging down her back. Everyone said how pretty she was, and Jay thought maybe she was, but she didn't look at all like him. He had black hair, and she had reddish brown hair and green eyes. She was tall for a woman, and thin, and he was thick through the body, like his dad. "It's a quarter to ten. You're forty-five minutes late."

"It seems like it's still early."

"That's because the sun stays up forever. I just hate setting the clock forward two hours." She glanced over at Grandma, who was sitting next to her, both of them on white wicker chairs.

The crickets had started in, chirping loud, but the sun wasn't gone yet, not all the way.

Grandma was nodding. "I know what you mean. When the sun finally goes down it's time to go to bed, and it's still hot as blazes." She fanned herself with her hand, the way she always did. Mom and Grandma said the same things to each other every night.

It was true about the heat, though. The middle of Utah was worse than Salt Lake, which was up by the mountains. Delta was in a flat place, with no mountains very close. In the afternoon there wasn't a cool spot anywhere, not even in the shade.

"You need a wristwatch, Jay."

He looked at the screen door and saw his grandpa standing there, sort of hidden by the dark screen. "Walk into my office and I'll give you one I don't use," Grandpa said.

"That's good," said Mom. "And then you'll have no more excuses. I'm not going to have this, Jay—you making promises and then running around all hours. This might be a little town, but there's still bad kids you can fall in with. What have you been doing?"

"Playing ball."

"Who with?"

"I don't know. A bunch of boys."

"What were their names?"

"Gordy and Lew and Eldred. I walked back into town with those three."

"They're okay, Louise," Grandpa said. "Gordy's the Linebaugh boy. You know his family. And it was probably Lewis Larsen, Jack's son. And little ol' Eldred Parsons; he's as good a boy as you'll ever find. His family just barely gets by, but they're good people."

"That's all well and good. But you know how

15

people talk down here, and you know the first thing they'll say about Jay. When I tell him to come in by a certain time, I want him to do it."

"What is it you think they're going to say?" Grandpa was asking.

"You know very well. He looks like his dad, and you know what people think about that."

That made Jay mad, but he only said, "I'll come home at nine from now on." Then he walked on into the house.

Grandpa had a room he called his office. It had been a bedroom once, when all the kids had been home—eight of them. His mom was the baby of the family, and Grandpa was over seventy.

Grandpa stepped to his desk and opened a drawer. "Everyone's wearing these wristwatches now. A salesman gave me one to try out, but I never remember to look at the thing. I always reach for my chain to pull my pocket watch out. I finally just stuck this thing in here. Do you want it?"

Grandpa wound it and set the time, and then handed it to Jay. It was silver, with a leather band. He watched the second hand sweep past silver dots instead of numbers. It looked nice, but he didn't want to wear it when he was playing ball. He took it, though, and he told Grandpa, "Thanks."

"So did you have fun with those boys tonight?"

"Sure."

He didn't tell about the ball that had hit him, but his throat still hurt when he swallowed.

"Do you think you're going to like living down here with us?"

"It should be all right."

"You'll get so you'll like everything after a while. It's just a little different from what you're used to."

He nodded.

"Well, if I were you, I'd go in and take a bath—so you won't be so hot when you go to bed."

"Okay."

"I don't mean you have to. I was just thinking that might be what you'd want to do."

"Okay."

After he walked out, he wished he'd said more. He liked Grandpa all right. He just didn't know what to say to him. And he didn't want him asking so many questions, the way he did sometimes. About Salt Lake and his dad and everything.

He played ball the next few nights, but he didn't talk much with anyone. Even when the boys played in teams and he had to wait for his turn at bat, most of the boys didn't say much to him. He never had been able to think of much to talk about. But Gordy never stopped talking.

He and Gordy were sitting next to each other on the grass one night when Gordy poked him with his elbow and said, "Hey, Chief, you ever seen a naked girl?"

Jay shook his head.

"We did. Me and Lew. We snuck up on some girls skinny-dipping down at the canal. We watched 'em for a while, and then we started hollering that we could see 'em, and they about drowned trying to stay under the water. But it didn't matter. They didn't have much of anything anyway."

Jay didn't know what to say.

"I seen my sister once too, just by accident. Now that I know what a girl's supposed to look like, I know it ain't like those flat-chested girls we seen down at the canal."

"What about Elaine Gleed?" Lew asked. "She's not so flat."

"What are you looking at *her* for? She likes me."

"You're the only one who thinks so."

"Yeah. Me and her. We're the only two." Gordy turned back to him. "Hey, you wanna go out to the desert with us in the morning? Me and Lew and some other guys are going out real early before it gets hot."

"I can't," he said. "I've got to work for my grandpa, at his farm."

"Is that what you've been doing every day?"

"No. Tomorrow's my first day."

"You must be starting up to cut hay."

"It's already cut."

"Then you'll be raking, and after that, hauling. Most of us do some of that. That's why we're going in the morning—before our dads get us busy doing the same thing."

Actually, he had done next to nothing since he'd been in Delta—except wait to head over to the ballpark late in the day. His mom had taken a job already, at D. Stevens department store, and Grandma was the only one home all day. He talked to Grandma sometimes. She liked to gab a little too much, but she laughed a lot. And sometimes he could think of things to tell her. But mostly he had read old comic books that some of his uncles had left behind, and he had tried throwing pitches at a big cottonwood tree out back, just to see if he could get better at throwing a ball where he meant to throw it—and maybe get so he could be a pitcher.

That morning, at the breakfast table, Grandpa had said, "Jay, I've got a boy from out at Topaz working for me at the farm. I've tried to get out there and help him a little, but I can't seem to find much time. I—"

"You shouldn't be out there in that heat anyway," Grandma had said. "You know what Doc Handley told you."

"Well, now, I guess I know what I can do and what I can't do."

"No, you don't. You never have known that." But Grandma was laughing, the way she did all the time.

Grandpa made a little motion with his hand, like he

was saying, *I'm not going to talk about that*, and then he set his hand on top of one of Jay's. Grandpa had big hands, all covered with spots, and his fingers were twisted at the joints. "I'm just thinking you could go out and give that boy—Ken's his name—a little help. I'll pay you for it, half a dollar a day, if you'd be willing to do that."

He could hardly believe it. That was a lot of money. He liked the idea of working, too, not sitting around. It was like being a man.

"You don't mind working with a Jap, do you?"

That took him by surprise. Why would Grandpa want him to work with a Jap?

"He's a nice boy, and he works like a demon. He'll keep you laughing, too."

He had known a Japanese boy in Salt Lake—a kid at one of the schools he'd gone to. But that was when he was little, way back before the war. Most Japs weren't like that boy. Japs were about the worst people in the world—except for Nazis. They'd bombed Pearl Harbor, out in Hawaii, for no reason at all, and that was pretty much the same as bombing America. They were ugly little yellow guys with glasses. He had seen lots of pictures of them on posters all over Salt Lake, and down here in Delta, too. Japs weren't as tough as the Marines, or anything like that, but they kept coming and coming, dying until they were stacked up like cordwood. They liked to torture people too. Gordy was right about that. What they wanted more than anything was to bomb California, and everywhere else in America after that. They wanted to take over the whole country, but Americans weren't going to let that happen. That's why they were fighting a war.

"Ken's seventeen. He just graduated. He's a good ballplayer—played for the high school out at the camp. You know about the camp, don't you?"

"What camp?"

"Topaz. It's what they call an 'internment camp.' It's out in the desert about twenty miles from here. After the war broke out, the government brought in over eight thousand Japs—a whole lot more people than live here in Delta—and set them up in barracks out there. They say that some of them are spies, and they want to blow up ships and airplanes, and do all sorts of things. But I don't know. They come in from Topaz on buses and shop at my drugstore sometimes, and they're all nice folks as far as I can tell."

That didn't sound right. Grandpa always liked everybody. Maybe he just liked to have Japs spend money at his drugstore. Jay didn't want to work with one.

Sometimes, in Salt Lake, boys had called him "Injun," and they'd made Indian noises, slapping their mouths and whooping. Gordy didn't seem to care if he was part Indian, but what would he say if he found out he worked with a Jap? Then he'd probably be a dirty Indian, not a Chief.

His dad had said things about Indians sometimes. Maybe he was half Navajo, but he made fun of Jay anyway—when he was joking around. "Hey, red man," he would yell, "don't scalp me," and then he would pretend he had a tomahawk and chop at Jay's head. But that was just joking. He liked to remember things like that now—when Dad was funny and playing around.

Mom had been mad at Dad way too much back then. But he was fun sometimes. That was what she always forgot. Once his dad had taken Jay up by the mountains to a zoo, and they'd walked all over and seen all the animals and everything. He'd even told Jay about things he'd done when he was a boy and had gone out to the Navajo reservation in the summer. He said, serious, he didn't mind being half Indian. His mother had taught him good things.

It seemed like Mom was still mad about everything. She remembered all the bad stuff too much. She hadn't even gone to the zoo with them. She should have done things like that, and not always told Dad what was wrong with him. He was a hero now, and when he came back, everything would be different. He wouldn't get mad when he got back.

CHAPTER 3

GRANDPA DROVE JAY TO THE FARM EARLY IN THE MORNING. IT WAS about a mile out of town. He introduced him to Ken, who was a little guy, no taller than Jay, but he had on a white undershirt with the sleeves rolled up high, and Jay could see what big muscles he had. He had tied a red bandanna around his forehead, and over that, had on a floppy old straw hat that was worn out and falling apart.

Ken started laughing, for no reason Jay could understand, and then he said, "I'm going to put some mileage on you today, Jay. Are you ready for some hard work?"

He sounded like an American.

"I guess so," he said, and he found out what Ken was talking about. The heat came on fast and got worse every hour. Ken had been cutting hay with a tractor for a few days, and it was bunched up in windrows. Now it needed to be raked and turned so it would dry all the way through before it was baled. Ken could turn the hay with the flick of a pitchfork, like turning pancakes, but Jay had trouble figuring out how to do it. After a couple of hours he was catching on better, but his back was breaking. The air was full of dried alfalfa, a million little pieces flying around. They were in his hair and ears, making him itch. The stuff was down his back, too, inside his shirt. It even felt like it had gotten into his lungs.

"What your grandpa needs is a rake a guy can pull with a tractor to turn this hay," Ken told him. "Most people don't do it by hand anymore." He straightened up and then leaned backward to stretch his muscles.

Jay hadn't said much to Ken all morning. He didn't want to start. The guy didn't seem like a Jap, but he was one anyway. He didn't wear glasses, and he didn't have big teeth, but he did look sort of like the guys on those posters—with the same kind of eyes.

"What he told me was, he doesn't cut enough hay to pay for something like that. I guess that might be right." And then Ken grinned. "It's okay with me. I need the money, and slow work is better than no work."

Jay didn't say anything, but he thought about that. He didn't like anything about this hay, but he wanted his mom to know, just by looking at him, that he'd worked hard. He'd buy his own school clothes this year, and that would be one thing she didn't have to worry about. It might put her in a better mood.

"Let me show you something." Ken jabbed his pitchfork into the ground and stepped over next to him. "You gotta raise the hay up higher, and then just flip your wrists, so you aren't making such a big motion with your arms. You're going to wear yourself out, fighting the stuff so hard."

He nodded. "Okay," he said.

"Go ahead and try it."

He stabbed at some hay with the pitchfork, got a good load, but as he lifted, Ken caught his forearm and forced him to lift higher than usual. Then Ken twisted his arm, so the pitchfork flipped over fast. Ken was right. It was easier that way. For a moment he was glad to know how to do it right. Then he thought about Ken touching him. He didn't like that. He didn't want the guy to start acting like they were friends.

"That's a lot better," Ken said. "Are you going to make it through the whole day?"

"Sure."

"I don't know. It's hot, and you're not used to work like this. If you have to knock off before the day's over—you know, just to rest up—I'll do your share for a while, and mine. It doesn't bother me to do that." Ken gave him a little punch in the shoulder and laughed.

"I can hold up," Jay said, and went back to work.

By noon the sun was straight above and burning Jay's bent back. Ken finally said, "Let's go sit behind the house and see what your grandma fixed us for lunch."

So the two walked to the farmhouse and sat in the shade of the willow trees out back. There were a couple of old wooden kitchen chairs out there. Grandpa had left their lunches on the back porch, in the shade, but there was no icebox to keep anything cool. Grandma had made a bunch of sandwiches out of baloney and cheese and they were about half baked by the heat, but they tasted all right. Best, though, was pumping up cool water from the old well, filling up a Ball jar over and over, and drinking it in long gulps.

"I'm not saying that I love to work this hard," Ken told him, "but one thing about it, right now a baloney sandwich tastes as good as a big old beefsteak."

Jay was thinking the same thing.

They were sitting close to a fat tree trunk, to stay in the shade. "How old are you, Jay?"

"Thirteen in a couple of months."

Ken laughed—deep in his throat, almost like a cough. "I guess you think that sounds better than 'twelve.'" He slid down in his chair, with his legs stretched out in front of him. He had eaten three sandwiches by the time Jay had started on a second one, and now he was holding his jar of water, resting it on his leg and then lifting it for a sip now and then. "What do you wanna do when you grow up?"

"I don't know." He thought he might walk into the house, or maybe say he needed to go to the outhouse. He didn't want to go back to work yet, but he didn't want to talk, either.

"I want to work hard now, then go to college so I won't have to work hard later. My dad ran a truck farm out in California. That's hard work, weeding those rows over and over, and then getting up early to pick and deliver the vegetables when they're nice and fresh. I never did like to get up early." He laughed some more. "But that's because I like to go out and cut a rug—you know, go out jitterbugging. My pop would roust me out anyway, and I'd be one tired customer—just barely in from bein' out."

He wasn't sure what to think of this guy. He didn't talk like the Japs in the movies—always saying "ah so," and that kind of stuff. And he hadn't known that Japs ever did the jitterbug.

"Do you like to dance, Jay?"

"I don't know how."

"What?" Ken raised his head. "At your age, I could already dance pretty good. Now me and Judy Okuba win every dance competition at the camp. The other kids just enter to see if they can come in second." Ken had gradually lowered his head backward onto the chair back. His eyes shut. "You want me to teach you some dance steps?"

"No."

"Why not?"

"I don't know. I don't want to dance."

"You will."

He didn't think so. He didn't like the way Ken bragged, either. That was one thing about Japs he hadn't known.

"Do you play any sports?"

"Baseball. The boys in town play just about every day—after it cools off a little." He wanted Ken to know that he had some friends.

"You any good?"

"Not real good." The heat was gathering under the trees, like it was swelling up the air. Crows were sitting in the trees and on the barn, but they weren't making a racket now. They were sitting still, like black, dried-up leaves on the branches.

"What position do you play?"

"I don't know. All of 'em."

"I'll bet most of the time you're out in right field, where they figure you can't do too much damage." Ken broke out laughing again, chugging like he had started a coughing fit. "No. I'm just giving you a hard time. But me, I play mostly shortstop. I made varsity in tenth grade back in California. Here at the camp, I lead my team in just about everything: batting average, runs batted in, runs scored. We beat everybody around here, easy—Delta High, Millard, all of 'em."

None of this sounded true. He didn't think a Jap

team could beat a regular high school team. Ken was just talking big again.

"I wish I could have finished school back in California. I went to this great high school in Berkeley, across the bay from San Francisco. Have you ever been out there?"

"No."

"I gotta tell you, it's the best. The kids were *cool*—that's what they say in California. We all went over to this one drugstore after school and we'd listen to the jukebox, maybe dance, or just talk to everybody." He was smiling, like he wanted to remember all that. Jay liked how he looked—wished he had some memories like that. "It's hard to believe I'm stuck in a place like this, so hot and everything. Out by our camp there's nothing but greasewood as far as you can see. The dust blows off the desert and right on through those tar-paper shacks we live in. You can hardly breathe when all that dirt is blowing."

"Can't you build better houses if you want to?"

Ken sat up. "Where have you been, Jay? Don't you know what's going on?"

"I just moved down here."

"I know. But there's a war on, man. And I'm Japanese American. People think we're on the other side. They rounded us up and *made* us come out here. The government calls it a 'relocation center,' but it's a *prison*. Guys with rifles watch us from towers. We're

Americans, the same as you, and we're locked up for no reason except that our families came here from Japan."

Jay nodded. He figured there must be more to it than that, but he wasn't going to say so to Ken. The guy was already sounding mad.

But Ken had started to laugh again. "I don't care, though. I'm making the best of everything. I'm going to join the army just as soon as I turn eighteen in August. We've got an all-Japanese-American combat team now, and it's going to get into the battle before long. I'm going to get into it if I can. Then I'm going to win me some medals and come home a hero. I'll have it made in the shade once I do that. I just figure if someone hands you a lemon, you make lemonade out of it. You know what I'm talking about? There's always a sunny side if you just look for it."

"I guess so."

"Life's what you make of it. That's my philosophy." Ken leaned back again, rested his head. His eyes shut.

Jay thought about telling Ken that his dad was a hero, just like Ken wanted to be. He wanted to say, "Japs took him prisoner. And I don't like Japs." Then he wouldn't talk to him anymore. He was almost sure that Ken was a liar. The guy wanted to act like he was an American and everything, but he wouldn't be in prison if there weren't some reason for it.

"You're not all white yourself, are you, Jay?" Ken asked.

He shrugged his shoulders, but he didn't answer.

"You're part Indian or Mexican or something, aren't you?"

"My grandma's Navajo."

"Okay. There's an example. Look at all the Indians stuck out in the desert on reservations. It's a lot the same. My name's Tanaka—Kenji Tanaka—so that's supposed to make me Japanese. But what about a guy named Gunther, or something like that? The guy who runs our camp is Mr. Ernst. That's a German name. Why don't they put him in prison for being German? You better be careful that someone doesn't say you've gotta live on a reservation because your grandma does."

"They don't do that."

"I know. I'm just saying. We were living in California, doing fine, and then Japan attacks Pearl Harbor and all of a sudden we're supposed to be the enemy. It doesn't make sense." He stared into Jay's face, like he wanted him to say that was right. Jay looked away. "But I'm not getting mad. I'm getting even. I'll fight for my country and show what I can do—and then I'll look any guy in the face and tell him, 'I'm just as much a man as you are. And I'm an *American*, right down to my little Japanese toes.'" Ken liked that. He laughed for a long time.

Jay had heard enough. He got out of his chair and lay on the grass. He shut his eyes and tried to pretend that he'd gone to sleep.

Not long after that Ken said it was time to go back to work, and before long everything was worse than in the morning. The heat was almost more than he could take—over a hundred, he was sure—and all the bits of hay floating around made him sick to his stomach. Ken got twice as much work done, and he never stopped joking, but every time he told Jay to go rest for a little while, Jay tried to work harder. He didn't know when quitting time was, but he knew he had to stick it out until then. His arms and shoulders and back ached so bad that he would slow down sometimes without knowing he was doing it. Then he'd see Ken watching him, and he'd speed up.

Finally Ken said, "Let's call it a day. We've got more done than I ever expected we could do." He took off his straw hat, pulled the bandanna off his head, and wiped it across his face. "Next time somebody tells me that Indians are lazy, I'm going to say, 'You don't know Jay Thacker. That boy can work like a man.'"

"I'm not an Indian," he said, but he liked what Ken had said about him. He walked the mile or so back into town, his legs shaking the whole way, and then got himself a bath. He was glad he'd made it through the day, but he was already wishing that he didn't have to go back again early the next morning.

After he washed up, he walked out to the kitchen and sat down at the table. Grandma didn't have dinner ready, but she was working on it. "Oh, Jay, you must be tired enough to go to bed right now."

"Just about," he said.

"I've got some of my grape juice in the cellar. Do you want to go down and get some? It's nice and cool."

"I don't think I can. My legs wouldn't make it."

Grandma laughed and so did he. Mom was grouchy about half the time, but Grandma never was. She was tall and skinny, like she was made of only bones and skin, and she had gray hair, but it was cut in her "summer cut"—almost as short as a boy's.

"I'll hike down and get you some in just a minute."

"No, I was just joking. I just want water."

"Well, get some, then."

"I already had so much it sloshes in my legs every time I take a step."

Grandma laughed hard at that. "Oh, Jay, you're such a funny boy."

No one else thought so, but he *was* sort of funny when he was around Grandma.

"I'm going to tell your grandpa, you should start early but not work so long into the afternoon."

"It's okay." He didn't want Grandpa, or especially his mom, to think that he'd been complaining.

"How'd you like Ken?"

"He tells lies."

"Lies? What lies?"

"He brags. He keeps saying how he's about the greatest thing there ever was. Dancing and playing baseball and everything."

"I know. He talks a little that way to me sometimes, but I think that boy's just trying to believe in himself. Things are hard for the Japanese people right now."

"Why are they out there at that camp?"

"I'm not so sure. I like those people. I go out there and meet with their book club. I take books out from the library and tell them which ones they might like to read. They treat me so nice, Jay, and every one of those women is just as ladylike as anyone in this town. More refined, if you want to know the truth."

"Ken doesn't think the government should've put them out there."

"Well, I can imagine he *would* feel that way. I guess it's partly for their own protection. Some people hate them so bad, they don't want them on the streets. They say they'll beat them up—or worse." Grandma was slicing potatoes, dropping the slices into grease in a frying pan, each slice making a sizzling noise as it fell. To him, it seemed way too hot to be cooking something like that.

He was still thinking about the camp. Something didn't sound right about it. "If one guy beats up another guy, it seems like the one doing the beating ought to go to jail—not the other way around."

Grandma stopped and turned around. "Now that's interesting you say that, Jay. I told your grandpa the same thing, and he said that in time of war things like that happen. It can't be helped. Maybe that's right. What do I know? But it doesn't seem fair to me either. Ken's a nice young man, and I don't see one reason to stick him out there in the desert in barracks so crowded that his family can hardly move without bumping into one another."

"Grandpa's probably right, though," he said. "Japs probably want to blow up airplanes and ships and everything. We can't take any chances with 'em."

"Well, maybe. That's what everyone says. They say there's some spies out there, but the ones I've met aren't troublemakers. They're just normal people, like anyone else. Grandpa says the same thing, but then he turns around and says it's probably what the government has to do."

Jay thought about that. Ken did seem like he wasn't too bad of a guy. But maybe he was just acting like that. A spy wasn't going to let on that he *was* a spy. He'd pretend like he was just some regular guy. Grandma probably didn't think of things like that.

"Gordy and the other boys said Grandpa's about the best man in this whole town."

"They said that?" She smiled.

"Yes."

"Well, he probably is. But he's wrong sometimes. And I oughta know. Because I'm the only one around here who's *always* right." She laughed at herself, sounding like a man, she was so loud.

Jay laughed too. He liked Grandma when she didn't get started talking about his dad.

CHAPTER 4

ON FRIDAY NIGHT JAY PLAYED BASEBALL AGAIN, BUT THE GAME WAS still going strong when he told Gordy that he had to leave.

"Hey, come on, you can't leave now. I'm not going to choose you anymore if you quit on us every night."

"I can't help it. I gotta go. It's almost nine o'clock."

"What are you, a baby? How come you have to go to bed at nine every night?"

"I don't have to go to bed. I just have to be home."

"Who says so? Your grandpa?"

"No. My mom."

It was a hot night, but a thunderstorm had blown through earlier, so the game had started late. The rain had left the field muddy and the air damp. He didn't mind leaving tonight. And he didn't mind leaving before he came up to bat next time. He'd been up four times so far and he'd only gotten one hit.

Gordy was standing behind the backstop with his fingers stuck through the chicken wire. Renny was up to bat. "Come on, knock one out of here," Gordy yelled. Without looking back at Jay, he said, "What's your mom's problem? How come she rides herd on you so hard?"

"I don't know." But he did know some things. His mom was trying to change. In Salt Lake she hadn't gone to church, and she and Dad had gone dancing sometimes and had come home smelling of smoke and beer. But now, she'd told him, she wasn't going to be like that. She wanted him to go to church, and she wanted him to be a missionary some day. She wanted him to do everything right, the way Grandpa and Grandma did. So he had to come in on time and be careful about the kind of kids he ran around with.

"It's not going to be dark for at least an hour, and you already gotta go home. That don't make sense to me."

"I know. But I better—"

"You wanna go out to the desert in the morning?"

"Yeah. Maybe. I don't have to work tomorrow." He hadn't ever said anything about working with Ken.

"So go with us. But you gotta get up early. We're leaving at six."

"I'll see if I can."

"What's that supposed to mean?"

Renny slapped a ball to the left side of the infield.

George should have fielded it, but he let it bounce off his glove, and then he tried to throw to second for a force-out, but he tossed the ball into right field. Before the mess was over, Renny had rounded the bases and Lew had scored in front of him. Gordy cheered them on, all the way around the bases, and then he said, "Stick around, Chief. You could get up again this inning."

But he didn't want to do that. "You guys'll be all right without me. See ya later."

"Okay. Six o'clock. We'll come by your house, so be ready. We're going to ride our bikes."

"All right," Jay said, but he wondered what kind of mood his mom would be in. Grandma said that it was making her upset, just waiting to find out about Dad. It was sort of the same for him. Every day he wondered if some kind of news would come, maybe that his dad was a prisoner of war. Sometimes the Japs let prisoners send a letter, his mom had told him, and maybe that would happen.

Mom had even said one time that Dad's body might be found, and then at least they would know. But it was wrong to think that way. Grandpa said they had to trust God and have faith, and pray to God that his dad would come home. So every time Jay thought maybe his dad was dead, he told himself not to think it, to have faith instead. And he prayed every night. He never had done that in Salt Lake, but he had started in Delta.

As Jay walked home, he decided he'd tell his grandma that he was going with his friends in the morning. She never worried about things like that, and his mom liked to sleep in late on Saturday mornings. She wouldn't know anything about it.

So that worked out all right, and Grandma even said she was getting up early to work in the garden before the heat came on. She'd get him up at five thirty and fix him breakfast. She even promised to pack him some sandwiches to take with him, the same as she did when he worked at the farm.

Gordy and Lew and Eldred came by in the morning. Another guy, Buddy, who played ball with them sometimes, came along too. Jay was standing out front, waiting. He had an old bike that one of his uncles had left at the house when he'd moved away. It was rusty and the chain came off easy, but it was the only bike he had. He saw the guys coming from a distance, all carrying their BB guns across their handlebars. The sound of their voices carried down the street. He didn't have a BB gun, and now he almost wished he hadn't said he would go. He didn't know what he'd do if they were all shooting their guns.

"Hey, Chief," Gordy called from a long way off. "I didn't think you'd show up."

Jay shrugged.

The boys all braked to a stop and put one foot down. "You got a gun?" Gordy asked.

"No."

"You can shoot mine."

"I thought we were going to look for arrowheads."

"Yeah. We'll do that, too."

They set out on their bikes, headed west out of town. There were farms all around, and he knew they'd have to go a few miles to get out to the desert. He just followed along, riding last and pumping hard to keep up on his beat-up old bicycle. After a while they turned off the paved road and headed down a dirt trail, full of ruts. It was still slick from the rain the day before, but that was better than a lot of dust blowing. The dirt was mostly gray out here, almost white. Grandpa said that that was from the alkaline in the soil, but Jay didn't know what that was.

The trail finally stopped at a barbed-wire fence. The boys all dropped their bikes. Gordy held the wires apart while everyone stepped through, and then they headed out into the desert. It was covered with sagebrush and greasewood. The land was flat, and to Jay, it was ugly. There wasn't much green out there, no grass except for some tufts here and there, and the greasewood was dry, twisted-up brush, like something starving for a little water. He watched the ground, wondering about arrowheads—and thinking a little about snakes. The boys worked their way through the brush, but no one seemed to be looking very hard. They were talking, or at least Gordy was, telling about what he'd heard on the radio the night before.

"Our air corps guys shot down fifty Jap planes yesterday. Something like that. I think they said *more than* fifty. If it keeps going like that, we'll wipe out every plane the Japs have. Their pilots don't have a chance. Our guys know how to fly a lot better."

"That's not what I heard," said Lew.

Gordy stopped and turned toward Lew. "What are you talking about?"

"The Japs have Zeros—that's what they call their fighters—and they're faster than our planes. They've got good pilots, too."

"Who told you that, Lew? That's a bunch of bunk. Japs can't even see good. Just about all of 'em have to wear eyeglasses."

"That's just how people draw them. Japs aren't all like that. I got an uncle who came home from basic training last week. He said they told him that Japs are good fighters."

"No, they're not. Your uncle's a chicken, that's all."

"No, he's not. He's already in the army, so he knows what's what."

Gordy stepped up close to Lew, so he had to look up to stare into Lew's eyes. "He don't know spit. He ain't been there yet."

"So? You haven't either."

Gordy turned away. He looked at Jay. "You wanna learn to shoot?" he asked.

"Me?"

"No. Your brother."

"Sure. I guess."

Lew was saying, "It's what he learned in training."

"Shut up, Lew. The guy's a chicken. I told you that already. See that rusty ol' tin can down there?" Now he was talking to Jay.

"Yeah."

Gordy took aim at it, breathed in, held still for a moment, then pulled the trigger. Jay heard a plunk and saw the can shake, and then Gordy said, "They don't call me 'deadeye' for nothing. I could kill more Japs and Krauts than anybody if they'd let me in the army."

He held out his BB gun to Jay. "Do you know how to aim?"

"Pretty much." He knew how to line up the sights. His dad had shown him how to do that with his cap gun—but only when he was just pretending to shoot. He took aim and pulled the trigger, but the BB kicked up dust about a foot in front of the can.

"You jerked when you pulled the trigger. That's the mistake most guys make. You gotta squeeze, not pull hard. Try again."

He concentrated this time, didn't hurry himself. He squeezed nice and easy and he heard a plunk.

43

"See. That's all there is to it."

"Yeah, but that can wasn't very far off," Buddy said. "Anybody could hit that."

"I know," Gordy said. "But a guy's got to learn."

"Not me. I was a natural, right from the beginning. Dad told me that."

"Hey, your face is what's natural. It looks just like my butt."

Jay couldn't help but laugh a little. Buddy's face was kind of ugly. It looked sort of puffy.

"Do you look at your butt a lot?" Eldred asked Gordy, and laughed. He twisted around to show how hard it was to look back there.

That made Jay laugh too.

Gordy was aiming again. And then he squeezed the trigger. Jay hadn't known what Gordy was aiming at until he saw a little splash of red on the top of a rock. Something flipped over into the dirt and then started wiggling around. The boys all ran over to it, and Jay followed.

"Come on, Gordy, you shouldn't be shooting horny toads," Lew said. "They don't hurt nothing."

"What difference does it make? There's millions of 'em out here."

"You just shouldn't do it, that's all."

Jay was watching the lizard, still twitching. Its legs were working, like it was trying to run, but it was on its back and most of its middle was torn away. Gordy didn't pay any attention to that. "Try that shot, mister natural shooter," he said. "A horny toad's a mighty small target, and I shot him from about thirty yards."

"Try twenty."

"No way." Gordy spun around and started pacing his way back, but then an argument started about where he'd been standing when he shot.

Jay was still watching the lizard. It had mostly stopped moving, but now and then it would jerk. Its blood had soaked into the dirt, just a brown spot. He thought of what his Navajo grandma had told him. She had come to Salt Lake a couple of times. She had worn long skirts, purple and blue-green, and she hadn't spoken very good English. One time he had smashed a spider, and she had said, "Don't kill. Not good to kill."

His dad had said, "Navajos don't kill anything unless there's a reason. For food, or something like that. That's probably how we all ought to be."

"What are you talking about?" his mom had said. "You kill bugs around the house all the time."

"I'm just saying that it's probably right, not to kill things for no reason."

Jay wondered if the horny toad felt pain. He wondered if there was a heaven for animals. His grandpa Reid had told him that every life had a spirit. Maybe that was sort of the same thing that Navajos believed.

He had been thinking about dying lately. He

wondered what it felt like to drown. He wondered if it hurt, and he wondered how scary it was. Gordy and the other guys liked to swim in the irrigation canals, and they had asked him if he wanted to go with them, but he didn't want to.

The boys stayed in the desert for a long time that morning. They never said anything about arrowheads. They just shot their BB guns. Even Lew thought it was all right to kill sparrows. "You shouldn't kill robins," he told Jay. "There's nothing wrong with robins, but sparrows are worthless. We have too many of them around. It's not bad to shoot barn swallows, either, especially if they get too thick around your place and they're pooping all over everything."

Jay hated that word "worthless." It was a word his dad had said sometimes.

"Nothing wrong with killing jackrabbits, either," said Buddy. "They eat up our gardens, and they carry sickness, like rats. We shoot at 'em with our BB guns, but they're hard to hit, and their hides are too thick anyway. If you hit one, you don't even know it for sure."

"I've killed plenty with my .22," Gordy said. "Me and my dad killed thirteen of 'em one day, and we sold the pelts over in Fillmore. Got ten cents each for 'em." But he was staring past Jay. "Okay, here's your chance. Look at those sparrows sitting in the brush over there. Shoot yourself one, Chief."

Gordy handed the BB gun over to Jay. He turned and looked at the birds. Gordy had let him shoot a few times, and it didn't seem very hard to do. But he had only picked out targets—cans and rocks and things. He didn't know if he wanted to shoot a bird. Still, he lifted the rifle to his shoulder so he didn't have to say anything to Gordy. He took aim at one of the birds that was sitting still. He pulled the trigger, jerked it really. He was surprised when he saw a puff of feathers. The sparrow leaped up, like it was going to fly, but then it rolled in the air and dropped behind the brush.

"Nice shot, Chief. Talk about a natural. You're a good shot already. You and me, we'll join the army someday and you'll kill as many Japs as me."

"We might have to kill us some right here in Delta one of these days," Buddy said.

He wondered if the sparrow was dead, or if it was trying to fly, maybe rolling around on the ground like the horny toad. He didn't want to go look.

"That's right," said Gordy. "You know about Camp Topaz, don't you, Chief?"

He nodded.

"There's about a million Japs out there, right out that direction." He pointed sort of north.

"It's only a few thousand," Eldred said.

"Well, it's a lot more people than we've got in Delta, and those guys want to get back to California to help the Japs from Japan drop bombs on us. They want to break out, a bunch of them, and then they'll need cars. They'll come into Delta and steal all the trucks and cars and everything they can get. And if anybody gets in their way, they'll just slit their throats."

"I know," Buddy said. "That's exactly what my dad says."

"They don't have guns out there at the camp. The government took them all away. But some of those guys hide away knives and stuff like that. Japs are sneaky, and if they can, they'll figure a way to crawl into your bedroom and cut your throat. Some guys I know keep a gun right by their bed at night. My dad's one of 'em. I keep my BB gun by my bed, and if one comes, I'll shoot him right between the eyes."

"That won't stop nobody," Buddy said.

"It will for a minute. It hurts, getting shot like that by a BB." He took his gun back and raised it toward Buddy. "Do you want me to shoot you in the face and see if it stops you?"

"Go ahead. But you do and I'll crack you over your head with the butt of my gun. That's what I'd do if a Jap came after me."

"Oh, sure. Laying on your back in bed. How're you going to do that?"

The argument kept going on like that. But Jay was thinking about Ken and the things he'd said about the camp—how the people out there were all Americans, the same as in town. And how he was going to fight for America. Maybe he was lying, but he was almost sure Ken wouldn't cut anybody's throat.

He looked out across the desert. Out far, the desert looked better, a shade of gray-blue, and there were gray mountains behind that. But it couldn't be a good place to live, out here. He could see what Ken was talking about.

CHAPTER 5

"NO!" KEN YELLED AT HIM. "YOU'RE REACHING DOWN FOR THE BALL, but you're not *getting* down. Your rear end ought to be scraping the ground."

"Okay," Jay said, just soft. He understood what Ken wanted him to do, but when the ball came at him hard, he was scared it would hit him in the face—or maybe in the throat again. The grass in the pasture was short, but the ground was lumpy. He didn't know what kind of hops the ball might take.

Ken hit another grounder, maybe softer, and this time Jay kept his mind on getting low. He watched the ball all the way into his glove. The ball took a hop to the side, but he shifted, and he gloved it just right.

"All right. Perfect. Now come up, set your feet, look at your target, and throw."

He cocked the ball and threw toward Ken, who had dropped his bat and was waiting barehanded. His throw was too high, though. Ken turned and chased it, but as he ran he yelled, "You're still trying to aim the ball." Ken found the ball in the long grass near the fence, picked it up, and turned around. "You can't be thinking that you might make a bad throw. You have to have confidence. Just look at me and fire away. If you try to aim, it never goes where you want it to."

Jay knew that, but he always worried that he wouldn't do things right. How was he supposed to stop thinking that way?

Ken kept hitting ground balls, though, and Jay was starting to field better than he ever had before. No one had ever told him the right way to do it. He made better throws, too.

After a time Ken said, "Well, we better get back to work. Our lunch time is gone. But you're getting better." He grinned at Jay.

"Thanks for helping me," Jay said. He didn't want to smile, but he did. Ken probably thought they were starting to be friends.

Ken walked past him toward the house, and he followed. He hadn't thought much about the heat when he was fielding, but he felt the trickles of sweat on his face now. "Didn't your dad ever teach you any of this stuff?" Ken asked, glancing back.

"Yeah, he taught me a lot of stuff. How to throw a football and everything like that. But I think I forgot."

Jay's dad had showed him how to put his fingers across the strings of a football. Jay had wanted to come outside and practice, but his dad had been drinking beer, sitting in the big chair he liked. "I'm too tired right now," he'd told Jay. "We'll do it tomorrow. We've got all day tomorrow." The next day was Sunday, and Dad had slept in late, and they never had gone out to throw. When he came back from the war, though, Dad wouldn't be like that. Mom had even said one time that the war would change how he was.

"Does your dad get any furloughs or anything like that?" Ken asked. He stopped at the back porch and set down the ball and bat. He picked up his jar, dumped out the warm water, and walked over to the pump. He filled it again and took a long drink.

Jay stepped into the shade behind the house. He didn't want to answer the question.

"Where is he exactly?"

"He was on a ship that got torpedoed. He's missing in action."

"Oh, man, are you serious?"

Jay saw the change in his face, the way his mouth came open. Ken felt sorry for him. But he didn't want that. He nodded, sort of shrugged, like it wasn't so important.

"Wow. That's rough. How come you never told me that?"

"I don't know."

"I guess you're worried about him."

"No, I'm not. He's going to be all right."

"Did you get word from him or something?"

Jay wiped his forehead and then put his hat back on. "No. I just know. He can swim real good." Ken was squinting from the sun in his eyes; his forehead was wrinkled up. "He told me when he left that he would come back for sure."

"What do you mean? Did he make a promise?"

"Yes."

Jay remembered the morning his dad had left, when he was getting on the train. "Don't look so worried," he'd said. "I'll be all right. I won't get myself killed." He'd laughed the way he always did, with his head back. "That's a promise."

That was what he'd said. Exactly. He'd promised.

He knew his dad wouldn't stop swimming, no matter what. And he wouldn't give up if the Japs beat up on him or even tortured him.

"So what is it you think, that he's a prisoner of war?" Ken let his hand drop. He looked down at the dirt. He was so thin that his T-shirt, wet with sweat, clung to his ribs, all of them showing.

"Probably. Or maybe he's on an island, hiding out." He didn't tell Ken about all the prayers he'd said.

"Being a POW is pretty rough. They don't treat people the way we do. They don't even feed them enough to get by on."

Jay stared at Ken. Didn't the guy know it was *Japs* who did that stuff to Americans? Didn't he know he was a Jap himself?

Ken finally pumped some more water and then put the top on his jar, and he pulled his work gloves out of his back pocket. Jay walked to the pump and filled his own jar. He took a big drink and the water tasted good. June was almost over now, and it seemed like the days were getting hotter all the time. In Salt Lake, summers had been hot, but never like this, and he had never had to work outside all day. He and Ken had started early that morning, at six, and they planned to knock off early—by three or so—but right now he could hardly stand to think of working for a couple more hours.

They walked back toward the field, the dust kicking up around them. "I know what you've been thinking all this time," Ken said.

"About what?"

"You're thinking I'm a Jap, just the same as the guys who maybe have your dad."

Jay couldn't think what to say.

"That's what everybody thinks. That's why people hate us."

He remembered what Gordy and the other boys had said about the people at Topaz.

"I can't do anything right," said Ken.

Jay tucked his hand in his pocket and just walked

along. He tried to act like he wasn't embarrassed or anything.

"I get it from both sides," Ken went on. "I walked into town yesterday, and the people I passed on the streets all turned their eyes away. I'd say hello to them, and then they'd look at me kind of crossways." He let his head swing and his eyes get big, to show how they'd looked at him. "They'd grunt or something, but they didn't want to speak to me. But I get caught on the other side too. My dad thinks I'm too American. He doesn't like anything I do—entering dance contests and all that kind of stuff."

Ken lifted the weather-beaten leather strap that held the gate shut. He pulled the gate back and let Jay step through before he shut it again.

Jay knew he had to say something. "How come he lets you do it, then?" he asked.

"I don't know. Things aren't like they were in Japan. Us kids don't do everything our parents tell us all the time. My dad knows that, but he doesn't say anything. I think it shames him to tell me something and then have me pay no attention, so he just stops telling me."

Ken walked ahead, with Jay behind.

"I'll tell you what, Jay. Everybody in this world wants me to be nobody, but I'm not listening. Those people on the street, they think I'm just a Jap, and that's nobody, and my dad thinks I'm not Japanese, so that's being nobody. But I thumb my nose at all of them." He made the motion, catching his thumb under his nose. "I'm going to the war, and I'm going to make a name for myself. And then I'm going to college, get a good job, and make some bucks. I'm going to look people right in the eye and say, 'You're talking to *somebody.*'"

Jay didn't know if Ken could do it. Maybe he was just bragging, like always.

Ken stopped. He turned and faced Jay. "Do people look at you funny because you're an Indian?"

"I'm not an Indian."

"Part, you are. And you look Indian."

"I know. But I'm not."

"Don't you see it in people's faces, though?"

"I don't know." He walked on past Ken. But then he admitted, "The boys in town call me Chief. Gordy does, anyway. But he's just joking."

"No, he's not. He's telling you you're nobody. But look him in the eye, man. Don't let him turn you into nothing."

Jay nodded. He thought of that word he hated: "worthless."

"Here's what you gotta do," said Ken. "Learn to play ball better than any of those guys. Then they can't say anything to you. They can't even think it."

He hadn't thought about anything like that. He just wanted to play good enough so the guys would like to have him on their team.

"I was the best player on my team back in California. Everyone made fun of how small I was, but I didn't poke at the ball like a little leadoff guy. I swung hard." He put his fists together and took a big swing. "I hit so many doubles and triples that the coach had me bat third, even fourth sometimes. And then I outdanced those same guys, and I could outswim them or outrun them, or out-anything-else them. Nobody called me names, either, because I'm like a wild dog in a fight."

He hadn't expected this. Ken was usually joking around, not mad. But his voice was mad now—hard as pavement.

"I'll tell you what else. I made everybody laugh, and everybody at my school liked me. I was vice president of my sophomore class. There were only about ten Japanese kids in my whole school, and all those white kids voted for me. You need to know that stuff, Jay—how to laugh and get along with every-body. Your trouble is, you don't talk enough."

Jay nodded.

"Why don't you speak up more?"

"I can't think of things to say most of the time."

Ken grabbed Jay's arm, made him stop walking. "Hey, tell some jokes. Kid around a little. People like that. You have to be one of the guys—you know what I mean?"

"Yeah."

"No, you don't. You're looking at the dirt again. Step up to guys and say something, have a little fun with them. Flirt with the girls. Tell 'em how good they look and all that stuff. That's what it takes."

"Okay."

"Okay, huh?" He waited until Jay looked up. "But you know you aren't going to do it."

Jay tried not to look away this time. He wanted to say that he would do it, but he doubted he could.

"Let me tell you the facts of life, Jay. Nobody's going to set the table for guys like you and me and then invite us to come in and eat. We gotta open the door and walk in, and we gotta sit down at that table and start gobbling up the food—whether they pass it to us or not. You know what I'm telling you?"

"Yeah."

"No, you don't. Look at me."

Jay looked in his eyes again, but now Ken was laughing. He slapped him on the shoulder. "You don't get it yet. You're just a kid. But you'll figure it out. Just remember what I'm telling you, and after a while, maybe you'll catch on."

Jay was nodding again, but that only made Ken laugh all the more.

Ken turned away and stepped up on the tractor, but before he started it, he said, "So those guys on your baseball team, are they good players?"

"No. Not very."

58

"I coach a team out at the camp. Young kids like you. Do you think they would play us sometime?"

"I guess they would."

"What do your friends say about us?"

"You mean . . ."

"Japs. What do they say about the *Japs* out at Topaz?" Ken was gripping the steering wheel of the tractor.

"I don't know."

"Yes, you do. I can see it in your eyes. Tell me the truth."

Jay looked out across the field. "They say some of you are spies, and you might want to go back and help the Japanese bomb California."

Ken laughed. "What else?"

"Gordy's dad said you'll need cars, and you'll steal them in Delta. You'll cut people's throats at night and then take their cars."

Ken laughed hard at that, but his voice was tight, not easy, the way it usually was. "What about Gordy? Does he think that too?"

"I think so."

"What do you think?"

"I don't think you'll cut anyone's throat."

"Hey, I might. Maybe I'll start with you. You better sleep with one eye open."

Jay finally smiled.

"So you and me—Jap and Indian—are we okay? You like me all right, don't you?"

Jay thought of saying that he wasn't an Indian, but it didn't matter. "Yeah. We're okay."

Ken tried to laugh again, but it didn't come out too well. "Do you know who those people are out there at the camp?"

Jay didn't know what Ken meant.

Ken twisted in his seat, then leaned forward with his gloved hands on his knees. "They're mostly farmers. Or they owned little shops. They don't cut people's throats. My dad is Japanese through and through, but his heart is broken right in half. He was making a go of things, running his little farm, and he could see how me and my sisters could do better here than back in the old country. Now he has nothing."

"Gordy and those guys were just talking, mostly."

"So what did you tell them?"

"Nothing."

"That's what I thought. Did you tell 'em you've been working with a Jap?"

"No."

"That's all right. I don't blame you. But look at me, Jay."

He looked up at Ken, who was still leaning down. "My dad would never hurt anyone. He couldn't do it if he had to. And that's how the other men are. They're not like me. If they came into town, they wouldn't say hello to anyone. They would get off the sidewalk and let people go by. I know what you hear about the Japanese army, and how they do things, but the people I know, the ones out at the camp, aren't like that."

Jay nodded.

"My whole family lives in a place sixteen feet wide and twenty feet long. Two more families live in the same barracks, and there's hardly any walls between us. If we were troublemakers, we'd be having riots. We'd be standing up for ourselves, saying we won't put up with that stuff. But everyone's just doing what they have to do to get by until the war's over. After that, no one's going to keep us down—at least not me."

Ken turned the key and pressed the starter button. The engine caught and started to grumble. "My name's not Kenji," Ken yelled over the sound. "Not anymore. It's Ken. I'm an American. If you tell those boys anything, you tell them that."

CHAPTER 6

"DO YOU CARE IF I PLAY IN THE INFIELD TONIGHT?" HE ASKED Gordy.

"Shoot, no," Gordy said. "Give it a try. You can't be any worse than Dwight. Play second base." Then he yelled to Dwight, "Play right field for a while. The Chief's going to give second a try."

"Hey, I'm a second baseman," said Dwight. "I don't like the outfield."

"It don't matter. Just trade for a couple of innings."

"Who made you the boss?" Dwight asked, but he was already walking backward, giving way.

"I ain't the boss. I never said I was. But fair is fair, you know what I mean? We might as well trade sometimes."

But Gordy *was* the boss. He knew it and so did everyone else. He was one of the captains who chose the teams every night, and his team always won. He always said he got first choice because he'd won the night before, and then he started by choosing Lew. Lately, he had started choosing Jay right after that.

Jay wanted to remember all the stuff Ken had taught him about fielding ground balls and throwing to first. Ken had been helping him practice his hitting, too. His stance was better, and he was learning not to swing at bad pitches. He had cracked a few long ones out at the farm.

He didn't have any ground balls come his way in the first inning, but he got up in the bottom of the inning and poked a nice line drive over the shortstop's head. Gordy would have stretched the hit into a double, but Jay didn't take any chances, even though he was pretty sure he could run as fast as Gordy.

"Hey, Chief, way to go," Gordy was shouting. "That's the best swing you've taken all summer."

Jay had driven in a run, too, and then he scored as the other guys kept hitting. When he returned to the field, right off, Albert topped a ball and sent a slow grounder toward the right side. Jay charged the ball, got low, watched it into his glove, spun and set his feet, and then threw to first.

The throw was a little high and Henry had to reach for it, but he made the catch. "Out!" Henry yelled, and so did Gordy, who was pitching. Albert thought he had beaten the throw, but all the guys in the field told him to get off the base, and his own team didn't argue much. Everyone except Albert knew he was out. Albert mumbled a few cuss words, but then he gave up.

Gordy walked over to him. "Hey, Chief, where'd you learn to do that? No one around here—except me—ever charges the ball like you're supposed to."

He didn't answer, but he was smiling a little. And in the next few innings, he handled most of the balls hit to his side. He bobbled one that he should have made a play on, but he made some good stops, and his throws got better and better.

When nine o'clock came, he didn't stop playing. He'd been pushing his time a little later pretty much every evening he played, and Mom hadn't been watching quite so closely as she had at first. She had met some of the guys he played with, and Grandpa was always saying they were okay. She seemed a little more settled down, too, not in such a bad mood all the time.

When the game broke up, it was almost ten o'clock. He and Gordy walked back through town. "What's going on, Chief?" he asked. "How come you're getting so good?"

"I'm not that good."

"Better than most of the guys. Have you been practicing or something?"

"A little."

"Who's teaching you?"

He wasn't going to talk about that. Gordy had found out that Ken was working for Grandpa, and he had said how bad that had to be, working with a Jap. Jay hadn't really agreed with him, but he hadn't dared to say that he didn't mind it too much.

"My dad taught me a lot about baseball before he went into the navy," he said. "I've been trying to practice a little and do what he told me."

"Who hits the ball to you? Patriarch Reid?" Gordy laughed at the idea.

"No. Sometimes I throw a ball at the garage out back, and then field it when it bounces back." That was true, but it didn't work very well.

"So was your dad really good at baseball?"

"Yeah, I think he was kind of a star in high school. He was good at football, too. He played in college."

"Then you're going to be good. Stuff like that comes down through families. My dad didn't play sports much, but he could break a horse when no one else could, and you've gotta be tough and have good balance and everything to stay on a horse when it's buckin'. Take you." Gordy started laughing, his voice scratching like a rusty saw. "You could probably shoot a bow and arrow like nobody's business, if you tried."

"I don't think so," was all he said. He was thinking, though, that he would tell Gordy sometime to lay off that stuff.

"Maybe what we should do," said Gordy, "is tomorrow night, not play a game, but teach all the guys how to play right. It sounds like you know what to tell 'em."

They were walking past the show house. A poster out front said what was playing—a stupid show with lots of girls dancing in fancy dresses. "I remember quite a bit," Jay said. "You're supposed to get in front of a ground ball, get your rear end down low, and watch the ball all the way into your glove."

"Now see, I didn't know that. Not about getting my butt down." Gordy stopped and tried the motion, maybe hunching down a little *too* low.

"You do it about right. I've watched you. You don't need to change anything."

"I'm a natural," Gordy said. "And I don't mean my face and my butt look the same." That got him laughing again. He gave Jay a little slug in the shoulder. Skin was still peeling off his nose and forehead. It seemed like he was always sunburned. "I was *born* knowing what to do. There's no stopping me."

"That's right."

Gordy stopped again. "I'll tell you what, Chief. Let's both work like crazy and get really, really good, and then let's make it to the majors—maybe play on the same team and everything."

"I doubt I ever could."

"Hey, don't say that. We can do it. We got the

ability, and maybe a lot of other guys do too, but we'll work harder than them."

Jay liked that idea. All of a sudden, it seemed like what he wanted to do.

"I'm good at basketball, too," Gordy said. He made a motion like he was dribbling, and then he pretended to take a shot. "Gordy Linebaugh sinks another basket!" he said, in a voice like a radio announcer. "That boy never misses. And they tell me all the girls want to smooch with him after the games."

Jay was laughing now. He couldn't help it.

"Did you ever kiss a girl, Chief? You know, someone besides your mother?"

"No."

"I kissed Elaine Gleed one time. I chased her down at recess, back in fifth grade, and I tried to kiss her on the lips, but she turned her head. She slapped me too. But at least I sort of got her. She says she doesn't like me now, but she does. Someday she'll be standing in line after a ballgame, just hoping I'll take her out and smooch with her."

Gordy walked all the way to Jay's house, even though it was out of his way. "Don't you have to get home?" Jay asked him.

"Naw. My parents don't pay any attention to what I do. I drive 'em crazy when I'm home. They say I talk too much. I don't know why they'd say such a thing. You never noticed it, did you?" He grinned.

It was turning out that Jay liked Gordy about as much as any friend he'd ever had.

When he walked into the house, he was a little worried. Mom was in the kitchen, sitting at the table with Grandma. "Aren't you awful late?" she said. But she wasn't mad. He could tell from her voice.

"The game was going good. I didn't want to quit and mess up our team." He had thought it over and decided that was how he'd explain it. It was true, too.

"Going *well*," Mom said.

He nodded.

"You told me before that it didn't matter if you left, that you couldn't play very well anyway."

He could tell that Grandma had been baking bread. The smell was thick in the kitchen. He liked seeing his mom this way—not so mad and nervous and everything.

"I'm getting to be a better player," he told her.

"Really?"

"Yeah. I got some hits tonight and made some good plays in the field. I'm the second baseman now. Gordy said I won the position by playing so good." He didn't dare say that he was going to make it to the major leagues.

"That's nice," Grandma said. "Have you gotten to like these boys down here?"

"Yeah. Pretty much."

Jay could see how pleased his mother was. She was leaning with her chin in her hand, but smiling. It was hot in the house, but she looked relaxed, like the heat wasn't bothering her as much as it had at first.

"Well, go get a bath," Mom said. "You've got dirt all over you. Once you're cleaned up, maybe Grandma will cut a slice of bread for you."

He noticed that his mother had been eating a slice of bread with chokecherry jelly. Grandma must have opened one of the last jars. She always said there wasn't much left from the year before, and not much sugar to make any this year.

Mom was smiling, maybe because she saw him staring at the bread and jelly, or maybe about his dirty shirt. She was wearing an old brown housedress she put on when she got home from work at nights, and her hair had come loose from where it had been wound up in back. It looked nice that way, especially with her eyes looking so soft. He wished she would be like that all the time. He remembered how nice she'd been, back when he was little. Back before so many things happened.

He took a bath and got his pajamas on, and then he ate his bread and jelly with Mom and Grandma. After, he went to his bedroom in the back of the house. There was a little air moving through the open windows, not exactly cool, but nice. Outside he could hear the crickets putting up a racket, the way they did every night. He didn't want to go to bed. He wished he could have sat around with Gordy for a while, and they could have talked more about making it to the majors. He liked what Gordy had said about him being a good player because of his dad.

Jay got out some comic books and sat on his bed. He'd read them all lots of times, but he thought he'd look through them again. After a while Mom showed up at his bedroom door. "Jay, you better get to sleep," she said. "Aren't you working in the morning?"

"No. Ken can't come over for a couple of days, and we got the hay all put up anyway."

"Well, that's good. I hate to see you have to work so hard all the time. You still seem like a little boy to me." She leaned against the door frame. She was still looking sort of peaceful.

"I don't mind working too much."

"I know you don't like to work with a Jap. I'm sorry you have to do that."

He thought about saying that Ken wasn't so bad, but he didn't. He rested his back against the head-board of the big old bed. Everything in the room was old-fashioned: the big chest of drawers, the table by his bed, the rolltop desk and chair—all of it made out of dark wood with fancy carving. He sort of liked everything that way. In Salt Lake, his parents hadn't had much furniture. They'd had to make do however they could.

"Well, anyway, you probably ought to—"

"Mom, was Dad a really good ballplayer?"

"You mean baseball?"

"Any sport."

She walked in and sat down on the bed, but she didn't twist around. She looked across the room toward the window, where the breeze was blowing the white curtains. "He played baseball, but he got into some kind of quarrel with his high school coach, so he quit. But I think football was his best sport anyway."

"Was he a star at football?"

"Well, I guess he was pretty good. He played at West High in Salt Lake, and then he made the team at the University of Utah. That's when I met him, when he was on the freshman team. But after that season, he decided to quit college and get a job. He just didn't have enough money to keep going."

"Did you graduate from college?"

"No, honey, I didn't. I about broke Grandma and Grandpa's hearts when I quit. My brothers and my sister all finished. Your uncle Max even has a master's degree. Not many people from down here go to college, but my parents always said they wanted us kids to go."

"Why did you quit?"

"I don't know. I didn't study the way I should have, and I didn't really like college that much. I finished my second year, but I was spending way too much time with your dad. He finally talked me into marrying him. Grandpa liked him all right, but he didn't think he was a very good choice for a husband, and I guess that made him seem all the better to me."

"How come?"

"I don't know, honey. Young people get to an age where they want to be independent. Anything their parents tell them *not* to do seems just the thing they want. Do you know what I mean?"

"I don't know." He was surprised. His mother had never said anything like that. It was like she thought he was growing up.

Mom twisted to look at him. "Well, don't get it in your head that it's a good idea. Don't be the way I was. I grew up down here, where things were pretty simple, but I got to the university and I started to think my parents didn't know much. Gary wasn't a Mormon, and that bothered Grandpa, but to me, he was exciting. He really knew how to have a good time. I hadn't ever known anyone quite like him."

Maybe later on she was sorry she married him. Jay thought about asking her if she had been, but he was afraid what she might say. "If Dad had stayed in college, do you think he would have been a star player?"

Mom looked away again, and he heard her take a long breath. "I don't know, Jay. He probably would have gotten into an argument with that coach too—or something would have happened. And then he would have quit. That happened to him a lot with the jobs he had. He'd do all right for a while, and then he'd get so he didn't like the people he worked for. He was out of work a lot. You know that."

Jay remembered that more than anything—how worried they always were about money. Dad was home a lot in the daytime, and Mom was the one at work. "He tried to find jobs," he said.

"Or at least he said he did."

"He did try. I know he did."

Her head came around fast. "Jay, you don't have to—" But she stopped. She turned back and took a breath. She didn't sound mad when she said, "Your dad was restless, Jay. Maybe he couldn't help that. But he always wanted some kind of change. And then, when he was feeling tied down, he would drink too much. You know how things were."

Jay did remember him drinking, and he remembered how angry his dad could get. And some of the things he'd done. "He didn't drink all the time," he said.

"Oh, no. I don't want you to think that. He could be the sweetest man who ever lived. And remember that big laugh of his? Remember how much fun we had that time we drove up to Yellowstone and stayed in those little cabins up there?"

Jay nodded. He loved to remember that trip. He and his dad had fished in Yellowstone Lake and caught big trout. He had a picture of the two of them, standing in front of the log cabin they had rented. Between them they held a long string of trout, some of them almost half as tall as Jay had been.

"Honey, we all have weaknesses. We all make mistakes. I'm trying not to remember so many of them. I want to remember the *best* things."

"He was nice to me. He taught me to play ball and everything."

Her head turned slowly toward him, and she gave him a long look—like she didn't believe that. She did that too much, always talking about the bad things Dad had done, even if she was talking different tonight.

"I think we have to learn from the things that happen to us, honey. And then do better. I want you to remember the good things about your dad, but I want you to be stronger. I want you to be more like Grandpa. Do you know what I mean?"

"I guess so." He watched the curtains blowing out, filling with air, then drifting back to the window again. It was good to feel some air moving in his room.

"You know how the people are at church. How they live, and how they talk and everything. Don't you want to be more like that?"

"Dad won medals in the war," he said. "Grandpa never did that."

"What medals?"

"You told me he got some medals. Because he was brave in the war."

"No, honey. It wasn't that. They were just what they call service medals—for participating in certain campaigns and things like that."

"You told me he was brave."

"Well, I think he *was* brave. But the medals weren't for that."

He tried to remember. He was sure that was what Mom had said. Now she was changing everything.

"I want you to be proud of your dad, Jay. He was willing to go and serve. We have to be proud of all our servicemen who are fighting for us."

"But he's brave. Not all those guys get medals."

She reached out a hand toward him. "Come here a sec." He didn't know what she wanted, but he crawled to her and she put her arm around him. "I just wish we knew for sure what's happened to him," she said.

He didn't like it when she said that. "He's all right, Mom. He can take whatever the Japs dish out. He'll come home to us."

"Maybe, honey. But I think we have to be ready for whatever comes. Do you know what I mean?"

He pulled back from her. "Grandpa said we have to have faith. I pray every night for him. You have to do that, Mom. You have to have faith too."

"Sure, honey. But people die in war. That's just the

way it is. Every family prays, but Heavenly Father can't bring all the boys home."

"Maybe some families have more faith. You have to pray every day. Grandpa said so."

"I do pray, Jay." She took hold of his arms, just above the elbows. "But part of faith is trusting God, honey. We have to accept whatever happens. I know you have bad memories from the way your dad treated you sometimes, and from some of the things he—"

"Don't talk about him that way."

"Jay, you know what we went through."

"He was nice to me. Lots of times."

"All right, honey. It's good you feel that way. You know that I love him too."

But she didn't really love Dad as much as she should. She shouldn't say those things about him drinking beer and losing his jobs. He was brave, and he was a star football player. He was a good father. "You need to keep praying," was all Jay could think to say.

"I do, honey. I do." But now she had started to cry. He didn't want that, didn't want her to go back to her sadness and her grouchiness, but she needed to know that he wasn't going to let her talk that way about his dad.

CHAPTER 7

THE FOURTH OF JULY CAME ON A SUNDAY, SO THE CELEBRATION IN
Delta was put off until Monday. Gordy came by for
Jay that morning, and they walked into town. There
was going to be a parade at nine o'clock that would
come down Main Street. He had seen the Covered
Wagon Days parade in Salt Lake; it had lasted for
hours. He couldn't imagine that such a little town
could come up with much, but at least some of the
boys had a few firecrackers, hard as they were to get
these days. Gordy said he was going to set some off
and try to scare some of the girls they knew.

When he and Gordy reached Main Street, it was just
after eight thirty, and not many people had come into
town yet. "Let's walk down the street and see if we can
spot Lew or any of the other guys," Gordy said.

"I know who you're really looking for," Jay said.

"Who?"

"Elaine Gleed."

Gordy turned and punched him in the shoulder. But then he surprised Jay by saying, "How did you know?"

"'Cause you love her."

"You can't blame me for that," he said. "The girl's a looker." He grinned with those giant front teeth of his, looking sort of goofy, but pleased with himself. "Have you seen how her and her friends have been coming around every night lately? I figure she's there to get a look at me."

Jay laughed. "I wouldn't bet on it."

"Why not? I'm the best player. Even a girl can tell that."

"Those girls are just looking around for something to do."

"Yeah. And maybe every one of 'em's got it bad for me. It wouldn't surprise me. In case you haven't noticed, I'm awful good-looking." He stopped and struck a pose, showing his profile.

"You're right about one thing. I *haven't* noticed." This was something new. Jay usually didn't joke much.

"You better watch it, Chief. You mess with me and I'll scalp you." He jumped and got him in a headlock, grabbed some of his hair, and pretended that he was hacking away at it. But Jay's temper fired; he swung him around and threw him off.

"Hey, Chief, what's up? You wanna fight a couple of rounds? 'Cause if you do, I'm ready for you." Gordy seemed about half-mad.

Jay wasn't going to let that happen. "You'd have a better chance fighting Elaine," he said, and tried to smile. "Try her first."

Gordy took a long look at him, like he wasn't sure whether he was mad or not, and then he started into that sandpaper laugh of his. "If she wants to go a few rounds with me, rasslin'—best two out of three—I guess I'd lock up with her. I might kiss her on the lips while I was at it too."

"She'd slap your face again."

"Yeah, she might. But then again, maybe that's just what she's hoping for—a little rasslin'. We're not kids, like the last time I kissed her."

Jay wondered. He had watched Elaine and Jolene Wickham and a couple of other girls. They'd actually paid no attention to the baseball game. They mostly seemed interested in talking to each other. They giggled all the time, the way girls always did, and he thought maybe sometimes they did talk about the boys. He had a feeling they made fun of Gordy.

Jay wondered what girls thought about him. Maybe they all thought he was an Indian, because of the stuff that Gordy always said.

The parade finally started, but it was a poor excuse for a parade. The mayor came by, he and his wife riding in the rumble seat of an old-fashioned Ford. The mayor was wearing a cowboy hat and using it to wave at people. And then a fire engine came along with a bunch of kids riding on it. He didn't know why that was in a parade. But most of the rest of the stuff was no better. They did have a couple of floats made on the back of hayracks, pulled by tractors. One had a tall guy on it, dressed up like Uncle Sam. Someone had painted signs and put them all over the sides of the hayrack, saying that people should buy war bonds.

The high school band marched down the street, and they played some pretty good music, nice and loud. That was about the best thing, except for a float with some high school girls on it—the Dairy Princesses. The truth was, two of them weren't much to look at—Gordy called them the "Dairy Cows." But the main one, the winner, was pretty. Gordy said she was Elaine's big sister, and Elaine was going to look just as good someday. "I'll take old Elaine to a dance sometime, and she'll wear a dress like that one her sister's got on—all low in the front—and I'll take a look right down her neck while I'm dancing with her."

"You better not let your mother hear you say something like that." Jay had been around Gordy's mother a couple of times now, and he'd heard her telling Gordy not to do this and not to do that.

"You're right about that, Chief. When me and Lew was in fourth grade, we tried to hide under the stairs, over at D. Stevens department store, and look up girls' dresses. We got caught doing it, and Mr. Stephens called my mom. I thought she was going to bust a gasket. But the only thing we seen was a big old lady wearing a girdle with all those straps to hold up her stockings. It made us both want to puke." And then he had to bend over and pretend he was puking.

Jay didn't need to see that, but he laughed anyway.

After the parade, he and Gordy found Lew and Eldred and some of the other boys at the baseball park—the nice one where the town team played on Saturday nights and Sunday afternoons. Some of the boys from the Delta High School team had gotten up a game with a team from out at Topaz. Jay was curious to see how well the Japanese boys could play, but as soon as he sat down in the bleachers, he noticed that Ken was out on the field, warming up at the shortstop position. That worried him a little.

Their coach was hitting ground balls to the infielders, and they were making some nice plays.

"These guys are good," Eldred said. He was sitting next to Jay, with Gordy on the other side, and Lew down on the end. Some other guys they knew were sitting in front of them.

Buddy turned around and said, "They claim they're in high school, but Japs all look younger than they really are. They're probably older guys."

Jay didn't say anything about Ken. He knew he *was*

out of high school, but just barely, and he was still seventeen.

"They'll do anything to beat us," said Lew. "Then they act like little banty roosters strutting around. All our guys that age are in the army. We could put a lot better team out there if it wasn't for that."

"Some Japs from out at the camp are in the army too," Jay said.

Buddy twisted more this time, to see who was talking. "What are you talking about? What army?"

"Our army."

"That's a big lie. My dad told me all about that. Some of 'em get into the army, but they don't fight. They just sit around at camps and don't do anything."

Jay didn't say anything at first, but he was sort of mad, so he told Buddy, "They're going to get into the fight pretty soon. They want some action, and President Roosevelt says he's going to give 'em a chance."

"What are you talking about, Thacker? Who told you that? That's nothing but a big lie."

He decided he'd better not say anything else. But Gordy got everyone laughing by saying, "Sounds like Chief wants to join up with those Japs. Maybe he can teach 'em how to fight with tomahawks. "

Buddy turned around again, grinning this time. "Is that what you've got in mind, Chief?"

"My name's Jay."

"Ooh. I better watch out. Chief sounds like he's about to go on the war path."

The boys all laughed again.

"Lay off, you guys," Gordy said. "Someday me and him are going to be major league ballplayers, and you're all going to brag you ever knew us."

"Yeah, sure," said Buddy. "And I'm going to sing like Bing Crosby and make a million bucks."

"Say what you want. We're going to do it."

Jay wasn't quite so sure as Gordy, but he liked hearing him say it.

The Delta team didn't get much going their first time at bat. The leadoff batter punched a single into right field and the crowd—especially the boys with him and Gordy—made a lot of noise. "Here we go. We're going to make these Japs look sick," Lew said. But the next batter knocked a ground ball to Ken, who made a great pickup, turned, and threw to second. The second baseman made a good pivot and threw out the runner at first. Double play.

All the noise in the bleachers stopped.

The next batter, Eldred's big brother, was supposed to be a great hitter, and he hit a hard grounder to the left side, but Ken broke to his right, fielded the ball backhand, and then made a strong throw to first.

"Man, who is that guy? He's good," said Gordy.

"Yeah, he's probably about thirty," Buddy said.

Jay kept his mouth shut, but as the team ran off the

field, straight toward the boys in the grandstand, Ken looked up at the bleachers and waved. "Hey, Jay," he said, "what did you think of that?"

He nodded but didn't say anything.

Ken stepped up to the fence. "Are these the guys you play with?"

He nodded again.

"How would you guys like to play against the team I coach?" he asked. "They're guys about your age."

No one spoke for a time, and then Gordy said, "Probably twice our age, if you tell the truth."

"No," Ken said, "they all have to be under fourteen for the league they play in at the camp. But we like to play someone else once in a while. Are you guys willing to take us on?" Ken was smiling, sounding friendly.

"How come you know Chief?" asked Gordy.

"Who?"

"Jay."

Ken took his hat off and rubbed his sleeve across his forehead. The heat was coming on now, feeling like a fire on Jay's back. "We work together on his grandpa's farm," Ken said.

"Oh, yeah. He told me about that."

"So, do you want to have a game?" Ken was looking sly, like he figured he had a better team than they did.

"I guess we could probably do that," Gordy said. "We'll have to talk it over."

"All right. I'll talk to Jay. We can figure something out. Maybe you could come out to the camp. We've got a pretty good field out there." Then he looked straight at Jay. "Your grandpa wants me back tomorrow. We can talk about it then."

"Okay," he said, but softly. He knew what was coming.

Ken sat down on his team's bench. Gordy whispered, "*That's* the guy you work with?"

"Yeah."

"How come he sounds like an American?"

He wouldn't look at Gordy. He just kept looking out at the field. "He is an American," he said.

Buddy was twisting around again. "Now I know who's filling Chief with all that stuff about Japs joining the army."

"You never said he was a ballplayer," Gordy said.

Jay shrugged.

"Do you think they have a good team out there?"

"I don't know."

"That guy's a liar," Buddy said, keeping his voice down. "If we go out there, they'll throw a bunch of high school guys at us. How old is that shortstop, Chief? Twenty-five?"

"No. He's seventeen."

"That's what he told you, anyways," said Buddy.

"Ken's seventeen. He just finished high school a few weeks ago."

"Sounds like you and him are big pals," Buddy said.

Renny laughed, and then, without turning around, he said, "A Jap and an Indian working together. They probably sleep in the shade all day and then complain they don't get paid enough. I don't think Brother Reid's getting his money's worth."

"Shut up, okay? We work hard," Jay said.

Everyone got quiet. But he knew he'd done the wrong thing. Renny had said it like he was only joking, and now the guys probably thought he was being a hothead.

The crowd didn't yell much for their own team after that, but that was because the local boys couldn't do much against the Topaz team. By the bottom of the third inning Gordy said, "Come on, let's go. This ain't no fun." The Japanese team was ahead nine to one by then and they had the bases loaded with no outs. As Jay walked away with his friends, he heard the click of a bat and knew some more runs had probably scored.

"Those guys are so little, you can't pitch to 'em," Gordy said. "Dan had to keep taking something off his pitches just to make sure he got the ball in their strike zones."

But it wasn't like that. Jay had watched Ken hit a couple of line drives, one for a triple, and both times the pitch had been up in his eyes. And he had run the bases faster than anyone on the Delta team.

Gordy told everyone they ought to walk over to the park, so they did. It was set up for a town picnic, and a lot of families had laid out blankets or were sitting at the picnic tables. Later in the day there were supposed to be three-legged races and stuff like that. "If they have footraces, I'm going to win me some money again this year," Gordy said. "Last year I took first place and won myself half a dollar."

"That's because I slipped on my start," said Eldred. "But I'll beat you this year. And Jay will too. He's fast."

He did think maybe he could beat Gordy. He had started stretching singles into doubles lately.

"Don't give me that, Four-Eyes," Gordy said to Eldred. "I can beat you any day of the week, running backward with my feet tied together. And if Chief tries to beat me, I'll tomahawk him from behind."

Eldred glanced at Jay, as if to say, *Don't let him bother you*, but he didn't worry about it. Gordy didn't ever mean anything he said. It was guys like Buddy and Renny who bothered him.

The boys were looking around—maybe looking for the girls their age, although no one said it—when Brother Roundy came walking up to them. He was their leader in the church MIA—the Mutual Improvement Association. "Hey boys, are you all coming to Mutual Thursday night?" he asked.

Mitchell Roundy was a married man, in his thirties, but he was a pretty good guy. At Mutual the younger boys mostly did Boy Scouts. They hadn't gone on a campout yet, but Brother Roundy was planning one for later on in July. Jay was looking forward to it.

"We'll be there," Gordy said for everyone.

"Well, good. I was thinking, you might've heard what's happening this week—and maybe not liked the idea—but I want you to come anyway."

"They want to teach us to dance," Lew said. "I told my dad we're not interested."

"There ain't no teaching me to dance," said Gordy. "People have tried. Of course, if you could team me up with Elaine Gleed, I'd wrap up tight with her and do my level best to improve."

Brother Roundy smiled at Gordy. "Just bring your dancing shoes Thursday night."

"I ain't dancing," Buddy said. "Not with the girls in our ward. They're all too ugly."

"Well, that's fine," Brother Roundy said. "If you don't want to dance with girls, we'll just let you dance with ol' Renny there. You two might look good together."

"Hey!" complained Buddy.

But Gordy said, "Yeah, and you can walk each other home after the dance—and stand on the porch and smooch."

Buddy was ready to fight about that, but Brother

Roundy grabbed him by the shoulder and pulled him back. "That's enough of that, boys," he said. "But be there on Thursday."

Gordy turned to Jay. "Are you coming, Chief?"

"Yeah, he's going to do a war dance," Renny said.

Jay gave him a look that said, *Don't push me too far.*

But it was Gordy who said, "Lay off that stuff, Renny. The Chief's had enough of it."

That made everyone laugh. But Gordy asked again, "Are you going to come?"

"I guess," he said.

"I'll show up, then. But I may not dance. I gotta see who I get for a partner first."

But Jay was thinking, the boys had said so much about him being an Indian, maybe no girls would dance with him.

CHAPTER 8

ON TUESDAY MORNING JAY WENT BACK TO WORK WITH KEN. THE farm had gotten run-down over the last few years. A second crop of hay wouldn't need to be cut until late summer, but there were plenty of other things to do. Grandpa wanted to raise some calves, but too many of his fences were broken down. The barn needed some fixing too, the old loft sagging from the weight of the newly stacked hay.

Jay didn't like getting up early, but he was used to working with Ken, and he kind of liked it. Ken knew all kinds of stuff that he would never hear from anyone else. He knew everything about California. He'd traveled down to Hollywood once, and he'd gone swimming in the ocean. He knew about high school, too, and about dating girls. Jay thought maybe he ought to ask him about dancing—and maybe get some hints, like he'd gotten about baseball. His mom had tried to teach him to dance once, and he had walked on her feet so many times that he hadn't wanted to try again—and neither had she. He still didn't want to dance, but he didn't want to show up for Mutual and not be able to do a single thing right.

He put it off all morning, but finally, at lunch, he said, "They're having a dance Thursday night, over at our church. I guess they want to teach all us boys how to do some steps. I'm not sure they'll have much luck."

Ken had finished eating. He was taking a rest on the grass under a willow tree, with his hands under the back of his head. "Why? Won't you boys give it a try?"

"I don't know. Maybe some will. I might not even go." He was leaning against the trunk of the tree, his head back and his eyes shut.

"Hey, man, you gotta know how to dance. When you get to high school, you'll feel stupid if you don't know how."

Jay opened his eyes. "Maybe I won't go to dances."

"But you'll want to."

"I don't see why."

"Are you nuts? Don't you want to hold a girl in your arms—some little Kewpie doll whispering in your ear how much she loves you?" Ken laughed.

"They don't do that, do they?"

"They do to me. They just can't help themselves.

After I spin 'em around the floor a few times, they think they're dancing with Fred Astaire."

Jay knew who Fred Astaire was. He'd seen him in a couple of movies his mom had taken him to. But the last thing he wanted was to be some kind of sissy like that guy.

"Hey, man, I remember how it was," said Ken. "The first time I went to a dance, all I wanted to do was hide somewhere. But I got out there and tried the steps, and pretty soon I was shuffling around all right. The girls at that age aren't much good either. They're as nervous as we are. But it turns out all right. You keep getting better at it."

"My mom says I have two left feet."

Ken chuckled. "Stand up. Let me show you the fox-trot step. That's all you need to know for now."

Jay didn't move. It was what he had been hoping Ken would say, but now he felt like he couldn't do it.

Ken was getting up. "Come on. You can just stand behind me and do what I do."

He got up.

"Let's get off this grass." Ken walked to the front of the barn where the dirt was packed down hard. He waited for Jay to catch up and then he turned away from him, reached out wide with his left hand, and made a crook of his right arm—like he was holding a girl. "Okay, it's easy. Left, right, together. Left, right, together." Ken did the same step Jay's mother had tried to teach him. "Just follow my steps and do the same thing," Ken said, glancing back.

He could do it okay when he was watching Ken, but he'd also done all right with his mom as long as she was just showing him. It was when she turned on some music and made him hold her like a dance partner that he'd had trouble. She kept saying, "Listen to the music," and that was what he'd thought he was doing, but he kept taking steps different from hers and ending up on top of her foot. Still, he followed Ken for a while and felt a little better, just remembering how the step was supposed to go.

"Have you got it?" Ken asked, and he turned around.

"Yeah."

"You don't sound very sure."

"It's a little harder when two people are trying to step together."

"Okay, then, take hold of me like I'm your partner."

"No, that's okay. I'll just have to—"

"Come on. I'm not going to grab you like a girl." He took hold of Jay's right wrist and pulled his hand onto his hip, and then he took Jay's left hand and stretched it out. "Okay, you lead. I'll follow."

Jay was embarrassed, but he started taking the steps. Ken took the same steps, and they didn't turn or anything the way his mother had tried to make him do. They repeated the steps ten or twelve times, just fine, before Jay broke off and said, "Okay. I got it now."

"The trouble is, you need to do it to music and get the timing right. If you want, we can go in the house and turn the radio on."

"No. That's all right. I'll practice some more on my own, and then maybe me and my mom can try again."

"Okay. But don't worry. If you can do as much as you just did, you'll be better than most of your friends." Ken was grinning. He didn't have his straw hat on, and his hair was matted down on his forehead from sweating all morning. Sometimes Jay didn't think much about Ken being a Jap, but he could see his eyes now, his skin, and he felt a little funny about everything. His friends had no idea that he and Ken talked to each other the way they did, sort of like friends.

"Let me show you something else that's cool," Ken said. "The jitterbug is almost the same step—except you rock back more on the 'together' step." He started doing it. "Left, right, rock back. Try it. Just give it some jive, that's all."

Jay knew nothing about jive, but he started to do the step, pretty much the way he'd done it before, not rocking back and forth all that much and not bent-legged like Ken. And then Ken grabbed his hand. "Spin under my arm," he said, and suddenly Ken moved forward and spun him. Jay passed under Ken's arm, but then stopped. "Pick up the step," said Ken. "Left, right, rock back."

He did the step a couple of times and was about

to stop, but Ken said, "You spin me this time," and grabbed Jay's left hand. Jay didn't spin him at all, but Ken twisted under his arm and came out on the other side. Then he kept doing the step, still holding on. He was laughing at the same time. "Hey, man, that's all there is to it. Now you know how to jitterbug. You'll knock some girl's socks right off. You're going to have a girlfriend before long."

But Jay had stopped. "I don't think we're going to learn the jitterbug at the church," he said. He took a step back from Ken.

"That's okay. I'm just giving you the idea, so you'll know where to start. If you want, I can show you another trick or two each day. By the time school starts this fall, you could be pretty good at it."

"Naw. I don't think so." Jay walked back toward the shade. He wanted to sit down for a few minutes again before they went back to work. "Why don't you just teach me some more about baseball? I watched you yesterday, and you're really good."

"Just like I told you." Ken grinned, like he knew he was a bragger. "When do you guys want to play our boys out at the camp?"

"I don't know." He sat down on the grass, but Ken was still standing up.

"How about Saturday, either this week or next? I could go out there on the bus one of these nights and get everything set up."

"Maybe. I don't know."

"Who does?"

"Gordy, I guess."

"I'll walk into town with you after work. We'll go see him."

Jay nodded, but he wasn't sure that was a good idea.

It was probably time to get back to work, but he hoped Ken wouldn't grab his gloves and his water bottle yet. He wanted to shut his eyes for a few more minutes. He felt sort of funny around Ken now. A guy shouldn't grab another guy like that and start twirling him around. It was embarrassing. Maybe Japs did stuff like that, but regular people didn't.

Ken walked over to the back steps of the house. He sat down and took a long swig of water from the jar he had left there. "Man, it's hot," he said. "We hardly did anything and I'm sweating like we just ran a mile."

"It must be over a hundred," Jay said. He shut his eyes, but everything still seemed bright. The sun was filling up the air with yellow heat, the shade just as hot as anywhere else.

"Out at the camp it always seems like it's about ten degrees hotter than over here—and colder in the winter—but this is about as hot as I've ever seen it."

"Me too." Ken was still over by the house. He must have wanted some rest too, but Jay thought of what the boys had said—the two of them sleeping in the shade, both lazy. He got up suddenly, grabbed his gloves, and walked over to Ken.

Ken looked up at him, maybe surprised that Jay wanted to get going already. But he didn't get up himself. "You'll be a good dancer, Jay. You're getting the idea already."

"My dad's a good dancer," he said, just to say something. "My mom told me that."

"My dad won't dance," said Ken. "Back in Japan, people didn't dance the way we do here, and he keeps mostly to the old ways. He didn't come to America until he was grown up. But my mom, she moved here when she was just a little girl. She learned to dance. She wishes my father would dance with her."

Jay had his baseball cap in his hand. He put it on now. It was his way of saying, "We better get to work," but Ken was still sitting on the back steps.

"My father doesn't understand my mother sometimes," Ken said. "And he doesn't understand the first thing about me. He doesn't have any idea why I want to join the army."

"I thought you were joining up as soon as you turn eighteen."

"I probably will." He waited for a time before he said, "My mom keeps telling me to ask permission from him. But every time I bring it up, he gets mad."

"Why?"

"I told you how some people feel. America won't

give us our rights, so why should we go out and risk our lives?"

"Is that what he says?"

"No. He doesn't say anything—except, 'No. I sign no papers.'"

"Maybe he's afraid you'll get killed."

"I know." Ken finally stood up. He placed his straw hat on his head and then jammed it down a little. "That's what my mother says, and I'm the only son. But I don't see much sign that he cares about that. Whenever your grandpa comes out here, I listen to the way he talks to you—like he's your friend or something. I saw him pat you on the head one time. My dad never does that."

"Grandpa's just like that."

"What about your dad? Did he ever pat you on the head or anything like that?"

Jay tried to remember. He couldn't think of his dad ever doing that, but he said, "Sure. Lots of times. And he used to take me to ball games." He could remember one time when his dad had taken him to a Salt Lake Bees game. They had probably done other stuff too. Everything just seemed a long time ago now.

"The only thing my dad asks me about is where I've been—you know, if I go over to the canteen at the camp, or if I go to a dance or something. That's why I like staying out here at the farm. Even if I'm all alone at night, I can listen to the radio all I want, and I'm not all cramped up in the same room with my mom and dad and my sisters."

Jay understood about things like that. "One place where I lived in Salt Lake, I had to sleep in the kitchen on a roll-away bed—because our apartment was so little. And some places where we lived, I had to sleep on a couch."

"No kidding? I thought you always lived in a nice place like your grandpa's."

He thought of the trashy little apartments where he'd lived in Salt Lake. He thought of the worry, his mom always wondering whether she'd have enough money for groceries. He took a first step away, but Ken didn't move, so Jay stopped. He told the truth. "My dad was out of work a lot. A real lot. Sometimes we hardly had any food. Mom had to call Grandpa about it one time, long distance, and he drove up to Salt Lake with the trunk of his car full of groceries."

"I guess it's good you had your grandparents to help you out."

He looked back at Ken. "Yeah. It was."

He was remembering what happened—stuff he wasn't going to tell Ken. Grandpa had parked in front of their apartment house with all that food, and he and Mom had started hauling it in. He'd handed Jay a package of graham crackers, and Jay had opened them and started chewing them down. But his dad had come in then, and he had cussed and swore at Grandpa. "We don't need your help," he kept saying—yelling. And Mom was saying, "I've got to feed my son, Gary. What did you expect me to do?"

"How come your dad was out of work so much? It seems like there are a lot of jobs these days."

"That was before the war. He joined the navy when the war started."

"Just to get a job?"

"No. He wanted to fight for America. He was brave. He won medals, too. When he gets away from the—from being a POW . . . and comes home and everything, I'll bet his picture will be in the paper—you know, showing him with all the medals he won."

"That's great. That's how it's going to be for me, too. They'll be talking about what a great hero I am. I'm going for the Medal of Honor. You win that and people know what you're made of. That isn't what your dad got, is it?"

"I don't know what his medals are called. But he's a hero."

"Well, that's good. He sure won't be out of work when he gets back."

"That's right." Jay breathed in the yellow air, started to turn again, and then decided to admit what he was really worried about. "Sometimes my mom and dad had fights. But when he gets back, he'll make good money and everything. And they won't fight.

We'll probably go back to Salt Lake, but we'll get us a good house this time."

"That's good, Jay. See, you've got something to look forward to, the same as me."

"But right now isn't very good."

"Why's that?"

He'd said too much already, but he said it anyway. "My mom's upset about everything."

"She's worried about your dad. That's all."

"Yeah, I know." But that wasn't it. She had her mind made up he was dead already. So did Grandma. They pretty much said that sometimes. Mom was mostly worried about what was going to happen to her without a husband and everything. She wanted to go to church and be like everyone in Delta, not the way she'd been in Salt Lake, but she was pretty sure she knew what people thought of her. He'd heard her tell Grandma that she'd made a mess of her life.

He didn't like to think of the worst: what he'd heard her say. "They look at Jay," she'd said, "and he looks just like his dad. That's all they think about down here. That I went off and married an Indian."

Grandma had told him not to worry about that. "He's a good boy, and that's the only thing they think when they see him. Give people a little more credit than that."

"All I know is, Jay better not do one thing wrong, or you can just about guess what they'll say about him."

He had heard all that one night when he was reading comic books out on the porch—heard it through the kitchen window when they hadn't known he was there. But he had prayed more that night—prayed that his dad was okay and would come home, and that he'd get a good job this time. And Mom would be happy. He'd asked Grandpa about prayer again, and Grandpa had said that God did answer prayers.

Ken finally started to walk. The two walked together toward the barn. "No one's too happy right now, Jay," Ken said. "The war gets to people. How do you think we all feel out at that camp, living the way we do?"

"Is your dad mad about that?"

"Mostly he's ashamed. That's how all the older people are. They didn't do anything wrong, but they're ashamed anyway—just to be locked up, you know, and to know what people think about us. But I'm not like that. I look people in the eye. I've got nothing to be ashamed of."

"If you go into the army, what if you have to shoot Japs?"

"They won't send us there. They'll send us to Europe. Everyone says that."

"But what if they did?"

"Then I'd shoot 'em. They bombed us, didn't they? They've got it coming."

"Maybe that's what your dad's thinking, though— that he doesn't want you shooting Japs."

"We don't say 'Japs.' We're Japanese. Japanese Americans. Reid is probably an English name, or Scottish, or something like that. No one tells your grandpa he's English and ought to go back to England, do they? Everyone in America came from somewhere."

"I know."

"Except your Navajo grandma. She could tell us all to get out of her country."

"But your dad came from Japan. Maybe he doesn't want you shooting Japanese people."

"I know. He doesn't. And I don't want trouble with my dad, but I need to make up my own mind. Once I'm eighteen, I don't need his signature. I can join if I want to. I've already told my mother that."

They entered the musty old barn, filled with the smell of the new hay, but filled up with the yellow heat, too, so bad it made Jay's eyes hurt. "Does she say it's okay?"

"No. She says to get permission from him. Then she cries. But I'll do whatever I want. That's how I am."

Ken didn't sound so sure of himself now—not the way he usually did. He pulled his hat off, wiped his face, then looked at the sagging loft. The two of them were supposed to fix it somehow.

CHAPTER 9

JAY AND KEN WORKED IN THE BARN AFTER LUNCH. BOTH THEIR SHIRTS were soaked with sweat. The smell was bad too, especially when they shoveled manure out of the stalls. Jay hoped that Ken would forget about walking into town to see Gordy, but earlier than usual, Ken said, "I'm calling this quitting time. Let's get out of here."

Jay didn't know if that meant they were finished for the day, but Ken walked toward the house and said, "Let me wash up a little, and then we'll head into town."

Jay sat on the back steps, and after ten minutes or so, Ken came out with a clean shirt on and his hair slicked down. "I'm so good-looking it scares me sometimes," he said. He was grinning. "No wonder all the girls are in love with me."

"They love the way you smell, too. Like cow manure."

Ken laughed like a whip snapping, and then he slapped Jay on the back. "Hey, Jay, you're learning. That's what I told you—crack some jokes sometimes. That was good."

He liked that he'd made Ken laugh.

"I did wash, though. Now I smell like lye soap. That's not much better than manure."

Jay tried to think of something funny to say about lye soap, maybe that it burned the dirt off, or something like that, but he didn't say it. Something else was on his mind. He was wondering what people would say if they saw him and Ken together in town, laughing and making jokes.

Gordy lived in the west part of town, over by the railroad tracks. Jay took a side street and stayed on the edge of Delta. He was glad they didn't have to cross Main Street, where so many people would see them. There were some kids out playing, and he saw a woman taking clothes off a line, but she didn't pay any attention to Ken. One old man, sitting on his front porch, did seem to stare at them, or maybe he was just stiff in the neck.

When they got to Gordy's house, he didn't go up on the porch. He just stopped out front and yelled, "Gorrrrrd-eeeeeee." That was what the boys in Delta all did. It wasn't like Salt Lake.

It was Gordy's mother who came to the open door. She was a little woman, round as a pumpkin. She was wearing a faded housedress that was frayed all around the hem. "He's out in back," she said. She sounded like Gordy. "Don't mind the way I look. I've been washing this whole day. Wash day came a day late, with the Fourth and all, but it seems like I had double to do. Gordy gets his clothes dirtier than any kid I've ever seen."

"He slides a lot when we play ball," said Jay.

But she had finally taken a look at Ken. "Hello there," she said. Her smile was gone.

"Hello, ma'am. My name's Ken. I work for Jay's grandpa."

She nodded. Jay could see that she didn't know what to say.

"It's a bad day for washing," Ken said, "but a good day for drying."

She only nodded again.

"My mom saves the ironing for Tuesday, early, so the heat's not so bad."

It was what most women did, Jay thought, but Mrs. Linebaugh didn't say so. She was still watching Ken, like he might do something.

"I moved here from California, and down there, it was cool most of the time. At least where we lived, down by the San Francisco Bay. Have you ever been in that area, ma'am?"

She was still watching him, maybe not hearing anything. "What is it you want?" she asked.

"Gordy and the other boys are thinking about playing ball against our boys out at Topaz," Ken said. "We've got some pretty good baseball teams out there. Yesterday the team I play for beat the high school boys from here in town. Maybe you heard about that."

She gave a little shake of her head, but she looked confused.

Gordy came walking around the side of the house about then. "Hey," he called. Then he saw Ken. He looked surprised too.

"Hey, Gordy," Ken said. "I hear you're the guy I need to talk to. I'm trying to get up a game with your boys, like we talked about yesterday."

"Gordy," said Mrs. Linebaugh. When he looked at her, she gave her head a little shake.

"It's not a problem, ma'am," Ken said. "Other teams have come out to the camp. I can get it all arranged. We have a good diamond out there, with a backstop and everything. We cleared the field ourselves. It's all greasewood out there, I'm sure you know, but we dug all that out. It's a good place to play."

"Gordy has chores," she said.

"When did you want to play?" Gordy asked, and that surprised Jay.

"I was thinking Saturday. I can go out tomorrow night, maybe, and get everything set up."

Gordy walked closer. "And you think your boys can beat us, don't you?"

Ken was grinning now. "It's hard to say. I haven't seen you boys play—except for Jay here. He's doing pretty good now."

"Gordy," Mrs. Linebaugh said again.

Gordy gave her a wave of his hand. "It's all right, Ma. Don't worry about it."

"I want to talk to you."

"It's all right. Really."

She hesitated, took one more long look at Ken, and then walked back into the house.

Jay wanted to leave. He didn't like her being upset like that.

"Don't worry about her," said Gordy. "She's never talked to a Jap before—never had one walk right onto our property."

Jay ducked his head, but he heard Ken laugh a little. "I know. I've gotten used to that."

"You talk like an American. I noticed that yesterday."

"What do you expect me to say?" Ken made a little bow, with his palms clasped together under his chin. "Aaaah soooooo."

That made Gordy laugh. "Hey, yeah. That's what they do in the movies."

"Listen, man, I'm from California. I'm probably the coolest guy you've ever met."

Gordy was grinning like he was watching a circus act, but he said, "You can play some ball, I'll say that for you."

108

"He's been teaching me," Jay said. "That's why I've been getting better."

Gordy was standing on the lawn with his arms folded, facing Ken. He was covered with dirt—maybe from working in his garden. He had a ragged hat on too. A felt one. It was too big for him and sank down all the way to his ears. "You never told me that before," Gordy said. "It was this guy who's been teaching you?"

"Ken. My name's Ken."

"You always said your dad showed you stuff."

"I know. But Ken's been teaching me this summer."

Jay watched Gordy get used to the idea, looking at Ken almost the way Mrs. Linebaugh had, and then he said something Jay didn't expect. "How about teaching me, too?"

"Sure. I could come over when you guys play at night. I could teach all of you some stuff."

"Most of 'em aren't any good, but me and Chief, we want to play in the major leagues. Do you think you could help us?"

"Sure. But making the majors, that's pretty tough."

"I know. But we're naturals. We can play. And we're going to work as hard as we have to. We'll make it." Gordy took the old hat off. His hair was sticking up every which way. He wiped his hand over his forehead. "Do you think they'd ever let a Jap play on a pro team?"

"He's Japanese American," Jay said.

But Ken said, "After the war, they will. I'm signing up for the army pretty soon. After I kill about a thousand Krauts, they'll let me do anything I want."

That made Gordy laugh. "Chief told me about some Jap outfit in the American army. Do they really have something like that?"

"You bet your boots they do. All Japanese Americans. We can fight with the best of 'em."

"You talk awful big."

"So do you."

Gordy liked that. He grinned bigger than ever. When his lips pulled back from his big teeth, he looked a little like a horse.

"So do you want to play on Saturday?"

"I sure do. I've been wanting to see that Jap camp. And I want you to see how me and Chief can play ball. But set it up for next Saturday, not this one. Our boys need more practice time. Will you still help us, even if we're playing against your team?"

"Sure. It's just for fun. I'll line the game up for nine in the morning, before it gets too hot. There's an early bus that brings people into town from camp. You could catch it when it heads back."

"Sounds good to me. My mom's going to scream like a shot rabbit when I tell her, but my dad'll say it don't matter. He don't like Japs either, but he knows we play ball with you guys, and nothing bad comes of that. The only thing I'm not sure of is all the other guys—and *their* mothers."

"And I know why. We just want to get all you boys out there at the camp and then we'll cut your throats. That's what we do, you know?"

Gordy laughed for a long time about that. "I never met a Jap like you," he said.

"How many have you met?"

"Not any. But I still haven't met one like you." Ken was the one laughing now, but Gordy said, "Can you start tonight, and work with our team?"

"I guess so. I could stay around town for a while."

"Maybe I'll tell Ma you're going to come in and eat supper with us." That got him grinning again. "She'd just die right on the spot, that's all. I'd have to call ol' Mr. Booker, the undertaker, to come over and haul her off."

"I'll go over to Mr. Reid's house. He might have a crust of bread he could share with me. What time do you fellows play?"

"About seven or so."

"All right. I'll be there."

Jay and Ken left Gordy's and walked to Grandma and Grandpa's house. Jay thought Grandma wouldn't mind if Ken came over. He just worried about getting there.

People did look at them, but Ken said hello to everyone—went out of his way to do it—and some acted like it didn't matter. Mr. Batcheldor, a man who came into Grandpa's drugstore a lot, looked at him and then Ken, and his eyes narrowed down. He didn't say hello when Ken said it. He didn't even say hello to Jay. Ken didn't care.

When they walked into the house, Jay said, "I'm home."

Grandma yelled from the kitchen, "I saw you coming up the walk. Is that Ken you've got with you?"

"Yes, ma'am," Ken said, and he stepped into the kitchen first. "I'm going to play ball with the boys tonight—maybe teach them a few things I've learned on the high school team."

Grandma was sitting at the kitchen table. She had some socks in front of her. She was sitting where the light was good, darning a hole in one of them. "Say, that's wonderful. Jay told me how good you are."

"Well, what can I say? Jay wouldn't tell a lie."

"You boys rest up a little, and I'll get some supper on before too long. You'll eat with us, won't you, Ken?"

"Yes, ma'am. I was hoping you'd invite me. Jay tells me what a good cook you are."

"I'll tell you what, Ken. You know how to spread the blarney, and I don't think you're Irish. Jay never told you any such thing."

"Mrs. Reid, certainly *I* wouldn't tell a lie—any more than Jay would."

"Maybe not. But you know how to spread on the lard, nice and thick."

"He jokes a lot," Jay said. "That's why people like him."

Grandma smiled. "I guess that's right," she said. "You are a nice boy, Ken. It's too bad you're stuck out there in that sad place."

Ken crossed his arms over his chest, like he wanted to look serious. "It's all right. I'm leaving soon, going into the army."

Grandma looked up from her sewing. "That's what Jay told me. I just hope you'll be safe."

Jay hadn't thought much about it until lately, but he didn't like to think about Ken leaving.

Ken went out back after that and sat on the back porch. Jay washed up, and then he went out too. But Ken was on the floor of the porch by then, sleeping on his back. Jay didn't say anything. He just sat in a chair and waited, and then, after quite a while, Grandma called them to supper.

Ken heard that, and he got right up. "I could eat an old mule—the whole thing—and finish off with a couple of watermelons for dessert."

"That's how I am," Jay said. "Maybe a mule and an old sow, too." But it wasn't very funny. Ken didn't laugh much.

They walked down the hall, and Grandma told them to sit down. "Grandpa's still down at the store," she said. "He's stuck there late tonight. Your mom just came in, though. She'll be in to eat in just a minute."

The boys sat down, and Grandma started filling up their plates with cooked carrots and parsnips and mashed potatoes. "I cooked a little ham tonight, but we don't have much left. Meat is getting scarce these days. Your grandpa killed a hog this spring, but it's mostly gone now."

Mom walked into the kitchen. Jay looked up and saw her stop halfway to the table. She was looking at Ken. He could see that Grandma hadn't told her.

"This is Ken," he said. "From out at the farm."

She didn't say anything. She stood in the same place.

"Sit down," Grandma said. "We were just going to say the blessing."

"I'm not hungry," Mom said.

"Now come on. Just—" Grandma started.

But Mom turned and walked out of the room.

Everything was quiet for a few seconds, but then Ken said, "I could leave, Mrs. Reid. I know her husband is missing. I understand about that."

"No, Ken. You sit there and eat. If she wants to go without, that's up to her."

So Ken ate, and Jay and Grandma did too. They didn't laugh much, though, and didn't even talk much.

After supper, he and Ken went over to the ball field early, still in the heat, but Ken hit some grounders on the smooth field, and Jay handled them pretty well. Gordy came walking over after a while, and then the other boys started showing up. They all looked surprised when they saw Ken, but Gordy told everyone that Ken was a good guy, and he was going to teach them how to play. Most of the boys didn't say anything, but Renny told Gordy, "I don't need no lessons from a Jap," and he left.

Ken didn't stay for the whole practice, but he talked up the game out at the camp, and the boys were all in for it. Then he said he'd better walk back and get some sleep. He was tired. By then, Gordy was telling Jay what a good guy Ken was. "He's not like a real Jap, though," he said.

"The people out at the camp are like that," Jay said. "Ken says they grew up in America, mostly. They didn't bomb Pearl Harbor."

"Maybe some of 'em are like that," said Gordy. "Some of the rest are looking to steal all our cars and trucks and everything. Everyone knows that."

Jay didn't say anything. Lew said, "That's what I've heard too."

But Eldred said, "My dad knows some Japs from out there. They're just like Ken."

The boys walked back to town, and then Jay went home. He hoped he wouldn't see his mother, but she was sitting on the porch, waiting. "I don't want you walking around town with that boy again," she said.

"Grandma didn't care if he ate with us. She said—"

"Never mind what Grandma said. You need to think about your father. What would he think if he saw you runnin' around with someone like that?"

"Ken's an American. He's going in the army."

"The sooner the better." She folded her arms. "You've got enough going against you, Jay. That's what you have to understand. People already have ideas about you. You can bet on that. You don't need to be seen with a Jap. Do you understand what I'm telling you?"

"Yes."

"Well, you better. We have to live in this town. And I have to go down to the store every day. By now the word's probably all over town—you two walking around, playing ball and everything, just like two peas in a pod."

He didn't want to talk about this.

Mom was all stiff again, like she'd been when they first moved down here. Her face looked hard, especially her eyes. "I don't think the other boys' parents are going to like it either. Don't bring him into town again."

"Gordy liked him," he said.

"Gordy doesn't have enough brains to fill a thimble, Jay. Don't go by that."

He nodded, then walked to the screen door. But he stopped. "Ken's my friend," he said.

"That's all well and good, Jay, but you don't—"

"And Gordy's not as dumb as you think."

She said something else, but Jay didn't listen. He walked into the house.

CHAPTER 10

ON WEDNESDAY AND THURSDAY KEN BROUGHT THE RADIO TO THE kitchen door. He turned it up loud and played dance music. Most of the time he danced in front of Jay and stepped hard to the music so that he could get the beat right. But when Ken found a hot tune, he would grab Jay's hand and show him some jitterbug tricks. He taught him some different ways to spin a partner or to twirl past her.

Jay still felt embarrassed dancing with a boy, but he liked the idea of showing up at the dance and not looking stupid. Ken kept telling him, "You're catching on. You're hearing the rhythm now, aren't you?" And he thought he was.

Ken took the bus out to camp on Wednesday night. That meant he didn't come into town to help the boys, and Thursday night was Mutual, so they wouldn't be playing. Jay was kind of glad about that. He didn't want his mom upset again. He did tell Ken, "I'm sorry about my mother."

Ken was pulling on some wire, trying to fix an old fence. He grunted as he said, "It doesn't matter. I'm used to all that kind of stuff. When a war's on, people like to hate someone. And this time around, that turns out to be me."

Jay stepped in and helped hold the wire while Ken drove a staple in the post. "What about Indians?" he asked. "Why do people hate them?"

Ken stepped back from the fence post and looked at him. "I can't answer that one, Jay. It's like everyone has to figure out someone not to like."

Jay couldn't understand that.

"Think about yourself. The first few days out here, you tried as hard as you could not to like me."

Jay didn't know that Ken had known that.

That night Jay walked over to the church by himself, but as soon as he stepped into the recreation hall, he saw Gordy with Eldred and Lew, standing about as far away from the dance band as they could get. Some of the band members were tuning up, and the drummer was still setting up his drums. A lot of kids were standing around in groups of four or five, girls together close to the band and boys mostly at the back of the hall. The weather had cooled off a little the last couple of days, but it was plenty hot inside the hall, even with all the windows open.

"Hey, Chief," Gordy said as Jay walked toward the boys, "what about the game? Are we on for next Saturday?"

"Yeah. Ken went out to the camp, and the boys out there want to play us. He said we can catch the bus in front of Van's Dance Hall and ride out there—so our parents won't have to drive us."

"My mother threw a conniption fit about me going out there, so I'll just take off that morning and not tell her where I'm going. She don't keep track of me anyways. The only way Dad'll get mad is if I don't get all my chores done."

"Do you think enough guys will go?" Eldred asked.

"Just so we get nine. That's all I care about. If Renny and Buddy don't go, we'll be better off without 'em." Gordy turned toward Jay. "Are you going to dance, Chief?"

"I guess. We have to, don't we?"

But Lew said, "What if we all say no? If they throw us out, we can go play ball."

"My mom and grandma said I have to dance," Jay said. And it was true. He had complained about going, but they had both told him he needed to learn to dance. Grandpa had joked about how a boy had to get himself "civilized" sooner or later, even if he'd rather be shooting rabbits or catching snakes.

"Maybe I'll just tromp real hard on all the girls' feet, and they'll tell me I'm too dangerous to dance," Gordy said.

"What are you talking about?" Lew said. "You said you wanted to come."

"No, I didn't. I just said I wanted to get my arms around Elaine. I don't want to dance with any of the rest of these girls." He looked at Eldred and laughed, then jabbed him a blow on the shoulder. "Should we do that, just tromp all over 'em on purpose?"

Eldred laughed, but he didn't say he would do it.

"Are you with me, Chief? Should we bust up some feet and get ourselves kicked out?"

"I won't have to do it on purpose. When my mom tried to teach me, I stepped all over her."

"You did it, though? You tried dancing?"

"My mom made me."

"Yeah. My mom too. But she's so round I told her we were doing the 'Beer Barrel Polka' and she was the barrel. She about kicked my pants." Gordy was laughing again, had never really stopped, and now some of the other guys their age were showing up. A guy on a horn, with a mute stuck in the end, was making weird sounds, and another guy was playing low notes, working up to high notes, on his clarinet.

Then Mitchell Roundy started yelling for everyone to quiet down and listen to him. He was dressed up in a white shirt and tie, with the sleeves rolled up, and his hair was slicked back.

"Everyone listen for a minute," he was calling out, and gradually the kids were getting quiet.

"Ol' Mitch went on a mission to New Zealand," Gordy said. "He can't talk to you three minutes in a Sunday school class without telling you one of his stories about it—like he was the only guy who ever went on one."

"Listen up now," Brother Roundy said. "We're going to start out with an opening prayer, and I've asked Sister Virginia Jones to say that. Right after she does, I want you older youth to move to the back part of the hall. When we start the music, you can choose up partners and dance. But you younger ones—all the Scouts and the Beehive girls—I want you to come up here to the front. We're going to assign you partners, and Sister LuRene Jenson, who's a professional dancer—"

"Don't tell them that," Sister Jenson called out. "I'm no professional. I just know—"

"Well, she might as well be a professional. She's taught dancing for many years, and she attended the BYU, where she took dancing classes from those teachers up there. She knows every kind of dance there is, and she can—"

"Stop bragging on me, Mitch. You're making my face turn red."

"Let's just leave, right now," Gordy said. "I can't listen to her screechy voice all night. She sounds like a magpie."

But Gordy didn't go anywhere, and Brother Roundy

was saying, "Well, you'll see. She knows what she's doing. Ginny, would you step up here by me and say an opening prayer?"

Ginny Jones was about sixteen or so, and she seemed pretty shy about the whole thing, but she stepped up by Brother Roundy, folded her arms in front of her, and said about the shortest prayer Jay had ever heard. But she did say something about everyone learning to dance "real well," and Gordy laughed about that.

Brother Roundy started in yelling almost as soon as everyone said, "Amen," and it still took him a good ten minutes to get all the younger kids up front and lined up in two lines, girls on one side and boys on the other. Jay didn't know how this whole thing was going to work, but Gordy seemed to. However much Gordy had talked about leaving, now he started counting girls in the other line and said, "Trade me places, Chief."

But it was too late. Brother Roundy saw what was happening and told Gordy, "Just stay in line where you are, Brother Linebaugh. You can choose your own partner later on." And then he had the two lines step closer together and there Jay was, standing in front of Elaine Gleed. She was thirteen, the same as Jay would soon be, but she seemed about two years older. To him she looked more like a woman than a girl. She had curly brown hair and eyes that looked bigger than fifty-cent pieces, blue as a lake. She was smiling for some reason, and that made her dimples sink in. He took one good look at her and then he was too embarrassed to look again.

"Okay, kids," Sister Jenson said. "I want you to take your partner, the one in front of you, by the hand." Her voice really did screech. It sounded like a dry wagon wheel. "I want everyone to spread out so you have a little room." The next thing he knew, Elaine was pulling him, walking backward, her hand gripping tight on his. She seemed to think she was in charge.

He took another glance at her. "Do you know how to dance?" she asked him.

He shrugged. "Not much," he said.

"I'll show you," she said. "I've danced lots of times."

He nodded. At least she hadn't told Brother Roundy she didn't want to dance with an Indian.

By then Sister Jenson was shouting instructions. The louder she yelled, the screechier her voice got. "We won't ask the band to play just yet. For now, we're going to practice the basic fox-trot step." He was relieved to hear that, and relieved when he heard her counting off one-two-together, the same as Ken had done. He knew he could manage that. When he started doing the step, he heard Elaine whisper, "Very good, Jay. Very good."

He hadn't thought that Elaine knew his name. He liked hearing her say it.

"All right. It's time for you boys to take hold of your partners." A mumble of complaint went up from all the dancers, but he wasn't paying much attention to any of that. Without looking into Elaine's face, he placed his right hand on her waist, the way Sister Jenson was telling the boys to do. Elaine was wearing a light blue summer dress, and the material was so thin it was like he was touching her skin. Elaine took hold of his hand before Sister Jenson even told them to, and he took another quick look at her. She was still smiling. "Don't be so scared," she said. "I'm not going to bite you."

He felt the tips of his ears get hot.

"All right now, still without the music—one-two-together, one-two-together."

The step was pretty much automatic for him now, but he knew his legs were stiff. All week Ken had been saying, "You're stiff as a scarecrow. Bend your knees a little. Move with the flow of the music." But he had never managed that.

"Very good," Elaine said again, "but you can get a *little* closer to me. It's hard to dance when you're reaching so far." She put a little pressure on his shoulder, and he felt himself hold back, but then she tugged harder and there he was, his nose only about four inches from hers. But now it was more obvious that he was shorter than she was, and he realized how much he hated that.

Sister Jenson was running from one couple to another, correcting, demonstrating, pushing boys closer, and all the while, never losing count. "One-two-together."

He was counting in his head, too, and he was keeping the step going, but Elaine said, "Let's turn a little. See, like this." Turns seemed to work better with her than they had with Ken, maybe because he had kept so much farther away from Ken.

"Wonderful, wonderful," Sister Jenson screeched. "This couple is doing *very* well. Elaine, you should be the one teaching, the way you've got your partner dancing."

He felt himself tighten up at the thought that others might be looking at him.

But Sister Jenson called out, "All right. You're getting the idea. Let's start the music. Boys, listen for the beat. I'll count in the beginning to help you, but remember, it's a matter of hearing the rhythm of the music, not just counting off numbers in your head. And *lead* your partners. Boys are supposed to lead."

He'd let go of Elaine and stepped back, but she leaned toward him and said, "I think I've been leading too much. You make the turns this time."

"Okay," he said without looking at her. He put his hand back on her waist, felt the warmth through the cloth.

And then she said, "I'm sure glad I got put with you, Jay. Most of these boys can't dance at all."

He felt something strange in his head—like maybe his vision was starting to cloud up. He took a long look at Elaine—maybe two or three seconds—and she nodded to him, still smiling. It was all more than he could believe.

The band began to play a slow tune, "I'll Be Seeing You." He didn't know all the words, only those first ones, but he liked that song, and he was holding her soft hand. She had moved even closer, as though their cheeks could touch by accident with the slightest wrong move, and he was turning on purpose—not a lot, not doing spins or anything, but not just holding straight all the time either. He thought maybe he was bending his knees a little too. He could smell something sweet and flowery coming from Elaine's hair, or maybe her neck.

Sister Jenson didn't let the band play very long—maybe a minute. Suddenly she stopped counting, and she must have waved or something to stop the music. "All right. Not too bad for the first time. But you boys, you dance like tin soldiers, all stiff. I want you to watch Elaine and . . . what's your partner's name?"

From somewhere in the room he heard Gordy yell, "It's Chief!"

But Elaine said, "Jay."

"All right. I want you two to demonstrate. Boys, watch Jay. He's got this down already. He looks like he's been dancing for years."

The band started to play again. He took hold of Elaine but stood for a moment, not sure when to start. He thought he missed the beat when he first stepped, but after a few seconds, he—or maybe Elaine—found the rhythm, and he continued his steps. He even started his turns, not feeling as smooth as before, but doing all right. And he kept getting better. "I'll be seeing you in all the old familiar places," Elaine was singing with the music. He wondered whether she was singing to him, or just singing, but everyone had moved back to watch, and he hardly knew it. He was just dancing.

Then the music stopped again. "Aren't they wonderful? What a beautiful couple they are. You give them a few years and they could be dancing in the movies."

He wanted to leave now. He was almost sure that he would mess this up. He just wanted to escape, without having to say a single word to his friends. But the music started and he was dancing again. "Dancing in the movies," Elaine said. She laughed. "Can you believe she said that? We're not *that* good."

He tried to laugh. But he didn't want to talk when he was dancing. He hadn't stepped on her foot yet, and he was afraid he would if he didn't keep his concentration.

"Where did you move here from, Jay?" Elaine asked him.

"Salt Lake."

"And you're Patriarch Reid's grandson, aren't you?"

"Yes."

"You probably did some dancing up in Salt Lake."

"No. This is my first time."

"But someone showed you the steps, didn't they? You knew them already."

He thought he'd lost the beat for a second, and he didn't answer, but after a moment he caught the rhythm again, and then he said, "My mom."

"She's a pretty woman. And your dad's in the war, isn't he?"

He nodded. And then he took a bit of a chance. "We think he's a prisoner of war."

"Really? That must be awful."

"He'll be okay."

He was watching her face more all the time now. She seemed ready to ask him another question when the music stopped. And then Sister Jenson asked everyone to change partners. For a while after that, maybe twenty minutes or so, she made them change again after every number, but he never did ask a girl; they all came to him. And every one of them told him he was the best dancer of all the boys.

And then Elaine came back. She took his hand and said, "I get you again, Jay. If I keep dancing with these other boys, every bone in my feet will be broken." She laughed close to him, her breath on his ear. And then they danced again, and he danced the best he had yet. "Dancing in the Dark" was the number, and she sang it, her voice small and pretty.

When the number ended, Brother Roundy started shouting again. "All right, kids. We're going to open this up for everyone now. But let's keep it going. You younger boys, don't make wallflowers out of these girls. Keep dancing, and keep choosing different partners so that everyone gets a chance."

But Elaine was still holding his hand. He would have walked away, but she didn't let go, and the music started. Now the band was playing a fast tune, "It Don't Mean a Thing." Jay turned toward her, and then words came out of his mouth that he would never have thought he could say: "I know how to jitterbug a little bit."

"Hey, my sister's been teaching me."

She grabbed both his hands, and they worked their way into the rhythm, left, right, rock back. He waited a while, but then he spun her under his arm. He didn't know too many of those kinds of turns, but he tried the ones he did know, and then he started over. By then the younger kids, who were still mostly at the front of the hall, had made a circle. They were clapping—or at least the girls were—and calling out, "Go after it!" and things like that.

At some point Jay had done everything he knew to do—five or six times—and he just wanted the music to end, but it went on much longer, and then Elaine spun into him, her back to his chest, touching him. It was a turn he'd never tried before. Whoops went up from the boys this time, and then Elaine spun back away from him. He took a good look at her, her face flushed, her hair swinging, her dimples showing. He had had no idea that he could ever feel this good.

Still, he was glad when the music ended. He knew he had pushed things as far as he could. "Thanks," he said to Elaine, and he turned and walked away, just to get out of the center of the circle.

Gordy hurried to him. "Hey, Chief, I can't believe it. How did you learn all that?"

Jay kept walking. He thought maybe he was heading for the doors, maybe even going home. He knew sweat was running down his face, and he at least wanted to get outside for a few minutes. But Gordy had hold of his arm and was spinning him around, and some of the other guys were gathering around him.

"Elaine's got it bad for you, Chief. She was smiling at you like you were Frank Sinatra. You got it made with her now—and all the other girls. I heard June Holbrook saying how *cute* you are."

Jay couldn't do this. He started walking again. "It's hot in here," he said.

But Gordy jumped around in front of him, stopped him. "How'd you learn to dance like that? Up in Salt Lake or—"

"He had a good teacher," someone said, a guy with a big voice.

Jay turned and saw a guy he'd seen around town, one of the high school boys. He knew what was coming, was almost sure. He thought about running for the door.

"Any of you boys could dance like that if you had your own personal teacher. A Jap teacher, at that."

Gordy spun around. "What are you talking about, Lester?"

"Tell 'em, kid. Tell 'em who you dance with out at your grandpa's farm." Lester was built like a long fence post. He was old enough to shave, with a shadow over his cheeks, but lots of pimples mixed in.

"What's he talking about?" Gordy was asking.

"I was driving with my brother out to our farm, and we passed by Kimball Reid's place. I looked over by the barn and couldn't believe what I seen. A Jap boy and this here kid—"

"What Jap?"

"The one who works for the Patriarch, putting up hay and fixing fences and all that kind of stuff."

"That's Ken," Gordy said. "He's all right."

"It ain't all right for two boys to dance together."

Things had gotten quiet, and Jay knew that the sound of Lester's voice was reaching around the hall. Elaine would hear this too.

"They were dancing together?"

"Yeah. We seen 'em. I guess this Indian boy likes Japs. And I think he likes boys more than he likes girls. That Jap had hold of him tight, like the two of them was fallin' in love."

"Sorry, Lester, but you got it wrong. That wasn't Chief. He wouldn't do something like that." But Gordy was staring at him, not at Lester.

Jay said, only loud enough for Gordy to hear, "He was just showing me how to dance, that's all."

"An Indian and a Jap, out dancing in the dirt," said Lester. "I thought I'd seen everything this world had to offer. But that was one I didn't expect. If I'd had a rifle with me, I'd have plugged 'em both. Something like that just shouldn't be going on around here."

Jay pushed past Gordy and walked to the door. He knew that every eye in the place was on him. When he reached the door, he broke into a run.

CHAPTER 11

WHEN JAY REACHED HOME HE STOPPED ON THE PORCH. HE WIPED his eyes and tried to get his breath under control. He didn't want anyone in the house asking questions. He pulled the screen door open and stepped into the front hallway. He heard a man's voice in the living room—a voice he didn't know. He thought maybe Grandpa was meeting with someone, so he walked fast to get past the entrance to the living room without saying anything.

But he heard his mom say, "Jay, is that you home already?"

He glanced into the living room and saw a man sitting on the couch across from his mother—a man he had seen at church. "Yeah, I didn't want to stay," he said. He heard his mom laugh and say something, but he kept going. He didn't know why that man was talking to his mother, but he didn't want to meet him.

He didn't like the way his mom had been laughing, sounding so happy.

He was hot from running, from everything. When he reached his bedroom, he pulled off his shirt and pants and lay on his bed in his underwear. A bit of air was moving through the window; he tried to feel it, tried to think what he could do now. He could stay away from everyone for the rest of the summer, but when school started, he would have to look at those guys. He knew what everyone would be saying.

Even if Elaine hadn't heard what Lester said, someone had told her by now. What was she thinking about him? "He learned to dance by dancing with a *boy*? A *Jap*?" People would tease her, too, and she'd be sorry that she ever danced with him.

They didn't know that Ken was just like them.

"Jay, honey, are you all right?"

He looked up. His mother was standing in the doorway. She was still looking happy, her face sort of reddish. She had lipstick on, and she had fixed her hair nice. She was even dressed up in her green dress with the stitching on the shoulder—the dress that she usually only wore to church. He didn't say anything. He wanted her to leave.

"What happened, honey? You seemed upset when you came in."

"Nothing happened."

She came to his bed and sat down, then leaned

toward him, with her hands on either side of him. "Your eyes are red. Have you been crying?"

"Who was that guy?"

"You know him, don't you? His name's Hal. Hal Duncan. He was a friend of mine in high school."

"A *boy*friend?"

"Yes. But that was a long time ago. He's been in the army. He was in the African campaign, in Tunisia. He got wounded over there."

"He looked all right to me."

"Well, he is. He's been recovering for months. But you're only asking me about him so I won't ask about you. Tell me what happened."

"Why was he here?"

"He just came to see me. We're old friends." But Jay could hear that her voice sounded nervous.

"Is he married?"

"No, he's not."

Jay stared at her, tried to see what was there. This was wrong, her laughing with some guy, maybe flirting, when his dad was a prisoner of war. Everything was wrong in this world. Everything. "I want to move back to Salt Lake. I don't like it here."

"Honey, you might as well know right now, we're never moving back. It's been hard for me to get used to things too, but this is a good place. I wish I'd never left it."

"That's not what you said before."

"I know. But I've changed my mind. I thought you had too. You've got more friends here than you ever had in Salt Lake."

"No, I don't. I don't have *any* friends."

"What happened? Did you get in a quarrel with Gordy, or—"

"I don't like Gordy. Or any of those guys. I don't want to live here."

"Tell Gordy you don't like being called Chief. I know that bothers you."

"I'll leave, Mom. I'll run away. I'm not going to live here."

He watched what was happening to her face, but he didn't care. She shouldn't have been flirting around with that Hal guy. She sat up straight, turned away from him. "We're not leaving, Jay. I made that mistake once in my life, thinking I had to get away from this little town. What I got away from were the things I was raised with. I made a whole lot of mistakes that I regret now. You know how bad things were for us."

He knew what she was saying. "We were okay."

"No, we weren't. We couldn't pay our bills. You know how we lived."

"Dad will want us to go back to Salt Lake when he gets home."

"Oh, Jay. Things aren't going to be like that."

He knew what she was saying. He heard it in the tired way she said it. "You think he's dead, don't you?

That's why you're flirting with that guy—looking for a new husband."

"Don't do this." She bent forward and cupped her hands over her face.

"He's not dead, but if you don't pray and have faith, he will be."

She turned back to him, and now her eyelashes were wet. "Honey, listen. We have to be honest with ourselves. His ship went down. No survivors were found. And now a lot of time has passed. We have to accept things the way they are."

He wasn't going to listen to this. "You want him dead. You want him dead so you can marry that guy." He sat up. "Get out of here. Get out of my room."

She stood up and looked down at him, her hands clasped together. "Jay, stop it. I've never seen you like this. Calm down."

"No. Get out of here. You hate Dad. You always hated him. You called him lazy. I heard you say that to him."

"We argued sometimes. I said things I shouldn't have, but so did he."

"You called him a lazy Indian. I remember you said that."

"I was mad, Jay. I just—"

"You're still mad."

She stepped close and looked right into his face. "Okay. I am mad." She waited, took a big breath, and then spoke in a softer voice. "He was mean to me, Jay. You know that. And he was mean to you. He's your dad, but yes, I'm mad about those things. If he did come back, we might not stay married anyway. You need to know that."

"He won't come back. You're killing him. Everything you say is killing him."

"That's stupid, Jay. He's either at the bottom of the ocean or he isn't. Nothing I say is going to make any difference."

Jay was crying—had been for a while. Everything she was saying was killing him. She had no faith at all. "Get out of here!" He slid off the bed, grabbed her by the shoulders, and tried to push her.

"Don't do that! That's what your dad thought he could do to me." She pushed his hands away.

"Get out of here!"

"Listen to me, Jay. You're lying to yourself about your dad. He *was* lazy, and sometimes he was mean. And don't talk to me about flirting. Your dad went out with other women. I caught him, and he said he wouldn't do it again, but he did."

"You hate him, so you're making all this up." He pushed her again.

She twisted away from him, then stepped back close, looked into his face again. "Jay, this is crazy. You want him to be a sports hero, and he wasn't. You want him to be a war hero, and he wasn't. You want him alive, and he isn't. We can't bring him back. And we can't make him into something he wasn't. I've tried to make you feel good about him. I thought you needed that. But he wasn't a good husband, and you know as well as I do, he was a *lousy* father. You know what he did to you."

"He was nice to me. He played ball with me. He—"

"How often? Once? Twice? The biggest mistake of my life was to marry your dad instead of Hal. Hal wanted to marry me, asked me every time I came home from college, and I married your dad because he was good-looking and exciting. But he was all show. You know that better than anyone."

"Get out! Get out!"

He pushed at her again, and she stepped away. "All right. But sooner or later, you have to stop making the guy up. And you're old enough to start—right now." She turned and walked out.

He was standing in the middle of the room, sweat running down his face, his body trembling. He didn't know what to do. He wanted to run away, but he didn't know how. He didn't know where to go, how he could live. He dropped onto the rag rug by his bed. He curled up, but he felt the heat of his own body, so he stretched out, ran his legs across the hardwood floor, searched for some coolness. He was crying hard now.

He was remembering things he tried never to think

about. His dad had spanked him a lot, had slapped him hard across his legs, his back. And he had screamed at Jay, called him filthy names, accused him of things, called him "worthless." Always that word. As a little boy, he had thought it was a curse word, some way of saying, "I hate you."

And he knew something else. One night, when Mom was working late, Dad had put him to bed early, but he hadn't gone to sleep. He had heard his dad talking to someone, heard his voice all slurry, the way it was when he drank, and he'd heard a woman laugh. Over and over she had laughed, and Dad kept saying, "Be quiet. My kid's asleep. You're going to wake him up." And then they'd both laughed.

He felt it more than remembered it. He didn't take time to think it through, the way he had so many times before. It was Mom who had told him that his dad would change, that he would come home from the war different. He still believed that. He had learned to say it to himself, repeat it when he remembered things he didn't want to think about. So what was she trying to tell him now?

He thought maybe he should pray—pray harder than ever. But he couldn't do it. He kept thinking of what she'd said: *at the bottom of the ocean.* He finally got up and lay on his bed again. He tried so hard most of the time not to remember, fought not to, but now he let the woman's voice come into his head, Dad telling her to be quiet, and the time his dad had got the razor strop from the bathroom and lashed him across the backside, making red welts that turned into bruises. And he remembered why: He had wet his bed. "Pee-pants," his dad had called him, and "baby," and "worthless," always worthless.

Grandpa stepped into the room. Jay felt him there before he heard him. He opened his eyes. "Jay, your mom's down in her room crying her eyes out. She wants you to know how sorry she is for the things she said to you."

"It doesn't matter."

Grandpa was wearing a white shirt and red suspenders. He had pulled the suspenders off his shoulders, and they were hanging over his hips. Jay looked at his middle, the white shirt, not at his face. "There's something I want to tell you," Grandpa said. He waited until Jay looked up at his eyes. "If I understand what happened tonight, you got upset about Hal Duncan coming over. But I just want you to know, I was sitting in the kitchen the whole time, just a few steps away. I could hear everything they were talking about. It's not like they were courting or anything like that. Hal's been your mom's good friend for many years—since grade school, actually. They talked about his wounds and his recovery, and they talked about their old friends. That's all that happened."

Grandpa didn't say anything about Mom wearing

lipstick, about being happy, about wearing her nice dress.

"Do you understand all that?"

Jay didn't answer.

"Do you?"

"Yes."

"Well, I just want you to know, your mom would never encourage another man so long as we don't know for sure about your dad. We know that things don't look good for him, but she isn't writing him off. She's married to him, and she'll be true to him until she knows for certain that he didn't survive."

"You told me to pray for him."

"Well, you should pray for him. That's what we all should do—ask the Lord to help him get through this if he happens to be alive and in a prison camp somewhere. But we also have to be honest with ourselves and accept that he probably went down with his ship."

"You told me not to give up."

He heard Grandpa breathing, long and smooth, as though he needed time, needed to think things over. Finally he said, "Well, it's good to hope for the best, but—"

"You told me to have faith and he would come home. You promised me he would."

"No. I didn't say that. I never made any promises. I told you to pray for him, and keep hoping. But I never promised anything. We have to trust the Lord. He knows what's best."

That sounded all upside down from what he had said before. Grandpa was going back on everything. That's how everyone was. No one ever gave straight answers or stuck with things they promised. He wanted to get away from this place.

"Jay, there's one more thing I want to tell you. I heard some of what your mom said when she was mad, and she didn't say it right, but it's something you need to understand." And now he waited again, breathed again, but Jay refused to look at his face. He stared at that bulge in the middle of him, the white buttons on his white shirt. "Your mom got to an age where she wouldn't listen to anything your grandmother and I told her. It was just one of those things some kids go through. Once she got to the university she stopped going to church, and I got back reports that she was running with a crowd of kids who weren't at all like her. I don't think she did anything too terrible, but that's what she meant when she said she left a lot of things behind—you know, the things she'd learned here with us."

Jay knew all that—knew that she hadn't gone to church in Salt Lake. He knew that she had gone drinking sometimes with Dad, gone out to dance halls, had smoked cigarettes sometimes, and he knew that she had stopped all that when they'd come back here.

"Your grandma and I met Gary, and we liked him all right, but then one day your mom showed up down here and said she was married to him. We weren't too happy about that, but—"

"Because he was an Indian."

"No, that's not true, Jay. He was half Indian, but that didn't matter to us."

"Mom said it did."

"Well . . ." Grandpa seemed to think that over. "Maybe it did some. I don't know. Some things run pretty deep in us, Jay, and a lot of people say things about Indians. But I tried to be fair about all that, and I liked Gary. He was a nice young man, handsome as any man you'll ever see, and he loved to sit out on the porch and talk with me. He even promised me he'd learn something about the church and consider whether he would join. But that was part of the problem, Jay, and that's what you mother was trying to tell you. The man knew how to say the right things, but there was always that other side to him. It wasn't until your mom moved back down here that I found out how rough he'd get with the two of you. If I'd known he was beating you and your mom, I would have gone up there and brought you both home."

Jay didn't want to hear about that again. He rolled away from Grandpa and looked at the wall. He tried to think how he could stop Grandpa. Grandpa needed to understand that Dad wasn't really like that. He got mad sometimes, and he'd hit his mom, but he was nice sometimes too. And when he came home from the war, he was going to be nice all the time. He was going to play ball with Jay and take him to ball games.

"Here's the thing, Jay. Hal Duncan is from a wonderful family here in Delta. He's as fine a man as you'll ever meet. He fell in love with your mom clear back in junior high, and he was true blue to her all the way through high school. When they went off to college, Hal went up to BYU and your mom to the University of Utah, but they'd see each other at Christmas break and times likes that, and he was always hoping she'd marry him someday. He would have been a great husband to her too. He graduated from college and had a good job up there in Provo. But he never got married all that time, and I know why. He was still in love with your mother. He just couldn't get her out of his system. He hasn't said that to me, but—"

Jay rolled back over, sat up partway. "You said he wasn't flirting with her."

"He wasn't. I'm not saying that. I'm just saying that he's not married. He's got a good job waiting for him, and his family still has a big farm down here that he can take over if he would rather do that. He's got a good head on his shoulders, and he's a soft-spoken, kind sort of man. You could get to like him, I'm sure."

Jay dropped back down. He felt stiff, like his muscles had all gone hard, his chest so tight it was hard for him to breathe right. "You told me to pray, but you didn't mean it. You want my dad to be dead so Mom can marry that guy."

"That's not true. But she does need to think about the future—and your future too."

Jay wasn't going to say anything else. He wanted to yell at his grandpa, the way he'd yelled at his mother—tell him to get out too. But he couldn't yell at Grandpa, not when he was talking so soft.

But Grandpa seemed to know all that without him saying so. "Jay, you get some sleep now. These things take some time to get used to. But it wouldn't hurt anything for Hal to stop by once in a while, the way he did tonight. And they won't ever be left alone. I'll make sure everything is kept proper."

Jay said nothing. Grandpa talked a little more, but it was all the same thing, just him repeating himself, and then he finally left. After Grandpa had been gone for a while, Jay slipped off the bed and onto his knees. He prayed the same prayer he'd prayed every night this summer. He asked God to bring his father home safe and well, and to change him so he would love his mom, and love him, and they would all be happy together. But all he could think of was the stuff his mom and Grandpa had said. What good did it do to pray, if they had given up?

CHAPTER 12

JAY THOUGHT HE WOULDN'T BE ABLE TO SLEEP, BUT HE DID. HE CURLED up on his bed without any covers and shut his mind off. He dropped like a rock into darkness. But he woke up early the next morning. The light was just a hint in his room. Gradually everything came back to him from the night before. He knew what he knew. His dad was dead.

He had known it for a long time, but now it was in his chest, like a weight on him. He didn't know if he could stand up, if he could walk, if he could get through a day. He wanted to play baseball, to go back to where he had been before the dance last night, but there was no way he could face everyone in town. Everyone in Delta would soon know the story.

He thought he might leave. He could hike out of town and then hitchhike his way back to Salt Lake. He had a friend there, a guy named Stanley White. Maybe

Stanley's mother would let him stay there, maybe sleep on the floor in the bedroom where Stanley and his brother slept. The idea seemed pretty good when it first came to him, but as soon as he tried to put it into words, plan it out, it fell apart. Mom would know right where to look. She and Grandpa would come after him.

Today, one way or another, the story about him and Ken dancing would get to this house. Mom would say it didn't matter, that everyone would forget about it. But they never would. He'd seen how Lester looked at him, heard him say that he should have shot the two of them. That was how people would feel.

The sun came on stronger, and then he heard footsteps in the hallway. He shut his eyes and pretended he was asleep. He heard his grandma's voice at the open door. "Jay, honey." She hesitated and then said, "What did you do, sleep on top of your covers?"

He didn't want to answer.

"Honey, are you going out to the farm? Maybe you don't want to go this morning. I know you're tired. If you'd rather just—"

"No. I'll go."

It was the best thing to do. He didn't want to be at home that morning and have his mom start talking to him again. He didn't want to see anyone. Ken was the only guy around who wouldn't know what had happened.

So he got up and pulled his old jeans off the chair where he'd left them. He didn't put on a shirt, just wore his undershirt. He laced on his work boots and then walked out to the kitchen. Grandma was making pancakes for him. He wondered what she knew, but then he saw it in her eyes. Grandpa had told her about his argument with Mom.

"Jay, honey, I know you didn't like Hal being here last night. But he's just lonely, the same as your mom. And they're old friends. It doesn't mean your mom's untrue to your father."

Jay sat at the table. He didn't want to talk about this. Grandma was nicer than just about anyone. She always thought everything would be all right. He watched her back as she flipped his pancakes over, her whole body making the motion, even her hips shifting. She was wearing a dress already, not a bathrobe like Mom would have had on. It was her gray dress—little black and white checks, really—and an apron over that. She was up for the day.

"Did you dance last night, honey?"

"A little."

"I'm glad you're learning. That's a skill you'll always be happy for, Jay. Some boys never learn to dance, and when they start to court a girl, they feel silly. It's too bad. Your grandpa's a wonderful dancer. When we were going together, he used to . . ."

On and on she went. She brought him his pancakes

and a glass of milk, and she never stopped talking. Everything was all right now in her mind. He ate while Grandma made sandwiches for him, and then he told her he was on his way. She took him in her arms and kissed him on the top of his head, pressing him tight against her bony body—tighter than he liked. Her apron was hot still, from the stove, and it smelled like flour and maple syrup. He pulled away quickly, walked to his bedroom to get his old baseball hat, then came back and grabbed the flour sack Grandma always put his lunch in.

He rode his bike down the street, hoping to see no one, but once he reached the Thompson place, on the edge of town, he pumped the mile or so down the road much more slowly. He was in no hurry to get to the farm. He felt funny about seeing Ken now. The guy never should have danced with him. He could have shown him the steps; he didn't have to grab hold of him.

When he reached the farm, Ken was up, but he was still inside the house. Jay walked to the back door. He looked through the screen, but he didn't say anything.

"Hey, Jay, I got up a little late. Come on in. Did you have some breakfast?"

"Yeah, I did."

"I'll just be a minute."

"I'll wait out here."

"No. Come in. I want to hear about the dance."

"That's all right. I'll just—"

"Come in. Come in."

Jay stepped inside and saw that Ken was scrambling eggs at the old electric range. The smell was filling the room—eggs and burnt toast.

Ken looked over and smiled. "So, were you a big hit? Did you show those guys how to do it?"

"No."

"But you danced, didn't you?"

"Yeah."

"And you did all right?"

"About the same as the rest." He turned and looked back out through the screen. He usually liked this time of day, before the heat came on, but the world looked dreary now, as though it would always be behind the dark mesh of the screen door. "What are we going to do today?" he asked, just to say something.

"Did you try any of your jitterbug steps?"

"No."

"What's the matter? You look all down in the dumps."

"I don't know." But then he added, "I want to move away from here."

Ken scraped the eggs from the frying pan onto a plate. Then he pulled open one side of the old toaster and grabbed a slice of toast that was almost black. He spread some butter onto it anyway, making a scraping sound and throwing little black flecks across the cabinet. He dropped the toast on his plate and set the plate on the wooden table. It wasn't until he sat down that he finally said, "I thought you were starting to like Delta."

Jay turned around. He thought of sitting down at the table across from Ken, but he decided to stay where he was. "I might go live with my other grandma," he said. It was an idea that had come to him as he had been riding to the farm. She was a nice lady who didn't speak much. She lived on a reservation in southern Utah, somewhere around Montezuma Creek. He remembered that name, and he figured if he got there, people could tell him how to find her. She would take him in.

"Are you talking about your Navajo grandma?"

"Yes."

"Would you have to live in a hogan, or whatever they call those things?"

"I guess so."

He hadn't really thought about that. He had only tried to think of somewhere he could go. If guys called him an Indian, well, he would go and be one. He would learn Indian ways. He would find out more about the desert than Gordy and the other guys would ever know.

Ken laughed. "I don't know, Jay. I don't think you'd like that. If you lived there, you'd have to learn some new dance steps, that's for sure. Maybe a war dance."

Ken thought that was funny, but it made Jay mad. He felt like telling Ken what he thought about his dance steps and all the trouble they had caused him. "I'm going to wait outside," he said.

Ken spoke with his mouth full. "Wait a sec." He chewed the hard toast, drank a quick gulp of milk, and swallowed. "I've gotta tell you my good news."

Jay waited.

"I took the bus back out to the camp again last night. There was something I wanted to tell my dad when I was out there the night before, but I lost my nerve. But I knew I had to do it. So last night I made him sit down with me, and I told him why I wanted to join the army—to prove myself and everything. You know, the stuff I've been telling you. I thought he wasn't even listening to me. He didn't say much. But then he said it was okay if I join when I turn eighteen."

Jay nodded.

"I think he knew I was going to go anyway, and it was just a way to save his pride, but that satisfied my mother—who's probably been talking to him, trying to convince him. My birthday's coming up in about a month. I've got to tell your grandpa I'm about to head out so he can find someone else, and I've got some other things to take care of, but I'm excited. In a few weeks I'll be in basic training somewhere. And then, look out, Krauts. I've got you in my sights." He held his arms up as though he were aiming a rifle.

"You don't even know how to shoot a gun," Jay said. He hadn't known he was mad that Ken was leaving until he'd said it, but he knew it now.

"Hey, what kind of burr got under your saddle?"

Jay didn't know. But now this was over too. Ken would leave, and he would be alone. There was *nothing* left here.

"I can shoot all right. And I'm in good shape already. I'll make those fat white guys at boot camp look like a bunch of boobs. I can't wait to get into a battle somewhere and rack up some kills."

"You'll get *yourself* killed. That's what you'll do." He was breathing hard. "And I don't care if you do."

"What?"

"You're a big bragger, that's all."

"You must have woken up on the wrong side of the bed, Jay. You—"

"You're like my dad. You think you're so great, but you'll get killed, just like him."

"You told me your dad was still alive."

"Shut up, all right? Just shut up."

"Hey, watch your mouth."

"My dad's dead. He's at the bottom of the ocean. He talked and talked and talked. He made promises. But he never kept any of them."

"Did you get word or something? Did they find his body?"

"No. But he's dead."

He was going to leave now. He wasn't going to talk to Ken anymore. He turned, but then he said what he'd wanted to say for a long time. "My dad was a big liar. Just like you."

Ken stood up from the table. "Look, that's enough. I don't know what's going on here, but you better lay off, right now."

"What are you going to do about it?"

"Don't try to find out."

"Oh, you're tough, aren't you? You're going to kill all those big Germans. But you're just a little *Jap*. The Germans will slap you away like a fly."

Ken stepped around the table. "I said that's enough, Jay. I may be small, but I'll fight like a man."

"Like a *chicken*. That's what Japs are. They're little yellow bellies. They torture people, and they . . ." But he couldn't think what else to say, what else he had heard his friends say.

Ken was on him by then, had hold of his shoulders. He shouted into his face, "Shut your mouth, Jay. If you weren't a little kid, I'd knock your head off."

"Go ahead. I don't care. You're just like my dad."

"Your dad was a drunken Indian. Maybe *he* was a liar, but I'm going to back up what I say."

"America's going to win the war," he shouted at

Ken, "and then we're going to ship all you *Japs* back to Japan." He waited for the blow. He knew it would be coming and he didn't care.

But Ken let go of him. "You've gone crazy, Jay. Just because your dad was no good, you don't have to put all that on me."

Jay charged him, thrust his hands into Ken's chest, sent him flying backward. Ken struck the table as he went down, shoving it back. The plate and the glass of milk flew. As Jay turned, he heard the sound of shattering glass, thought he saw the yellow scraps of egg fly. But he didn't care. He was falling off a cliff. He slammed his hand into the screen door, felt the old screen tear, and then felt the door pop open, and by then he was already running through, heading toward the barn and then on by. He didn't know where he was going from there, only that he couldn't go back to Delta.

"You'll be dead too," he yelled at the field in front of him. "You'll tell everyone what a hotshot you are, then get yourself killed. But I don't care."

He kept running. "I don't care," he shouted again. "I don't care."

CHAPTER 13

HE RAN UNTIL HIS LUNGS WOULDN'T LET HIM RUN ANYMORE, AND then he walked hard. He headed south from the farm, away from Delta, down a dirt road. He knew that he had to figure something out. He had to get away from Ken, and he was not going back to face the boys in town. He also wasn't going to watch his mother sit in the living room with Hal Duncan every night.

The road kept going until it gradually dwindled down to nothing more than tracks in the desert overgrown with rabbitbrush and mustard weed. It was stupid to keep heading deeper into the desert, but he couldn't think what else to do. He could head off to the east and try to get to a highway, maybe hitchhike his way somewhere. But he didn't know where. No matter what he'd said earlier, he couldn't really go to his Navajo grandmother. He didn't want to live in a hogan.

Jay stopped and looked out across the desert. Everything was flat and empty. It was gray more than green, and he didn't understand anything about it. Maybe Indians knew these places. Maybe they knew how to live out here, but he didn't. He needed to think of something else.

Maybe he really could make it to the major leagues. Maybe he could work harder than anyone and get really good. Gordy would probably never work that hard, but he thought he could. He needed to get to a place where he could practice every day, play on a good team, spend all his time getting better. If he could do something like that, someday no one in Delta would talk about him dancing with a Jap. They would say, "I knew that guy back when he lived here. He's a big-league ballplayer now."

He stopped. He looked out toward the mountains. Then he looked back toward Delta. Maybe he would have to go back to town—hide out there somehow while he figured things out. But he saw something moving, something black. He realized it was a train pulling out of town, the engine making black smoke. It would pass him by, to the west, but not by more than a quarter of a mile, and it didn't look like it was picking up much speed. He didn't know where it was going, but it was heading south, away from here.

He had seen hoboes in town. Grandma had fed them. He'd heard them say that they "rode the rails."

They jumped onto empty boxcars. Suddenly he was running. Lots of things were coming together in his mind. Maybe he could ride trains and get to California. There were jobs in California. He could say he was older than he was, get a job, then practice baseball every day after work. He wouldn't have to go back to town. But the train was going faster now, and he kept running harder and harder.

He didn't zig and zag much; he mostly crashed through the rabbitbrush, or jumped over it when he could, and he angled toward the train, cutting somewhat south to get to the middle of it before it left him behind. His lungs were aching again. He stumbled and went down but was up without losing much time or speed, running again and then getting close before he realized he didn't know how to get on. He saw ladders on the sides of the boxcars. He could jump onto them, but then what?

And then he saw an open door and jumped. He tried to jump onto the floor of the car but only got his shoulders through. He fought to get hold of something. He grabbed the side of the door, with his elbow against the inside. He clung hard but was dangling, couldn't pull himself up, and he knew he was in big trouble. He couldn't hang on forever, and he couldn't get any leverage to pull himself up.

Then suddenly something seized his arm and pulled, and he was swept inside the boxcar. Everything was dark for a moment, and he wasn't sure what had happened, but he rolled over and looked up at a hulking form, a man, standing over him. "You trying to git yerself killt?" the man said. His voice was like an echo from inside a barrel.

Jay didn't answer. He just stared up at the man, whose face he could see now. It was dark, covered with whiskers, with hair too long falling around his ears, and black eyebrows like thistles.

"He's just a kid," someone else said. Jay looked into the dark end of the car and saw two men sitting side by side, leaning back against rolls of blankets. His eyes were getting used to the dim light, and he could see that they were dirty, one in overalls, the other in tattered jeans, but they didn't look mean—or angry.

"You better hop back offa here," the big guy standing over him said. "Before we pick up too much speed."

He couldn't think what to say. But maybe he *should* jump off.

"You just playin' around?" one of the men sitting down asked, yelled really. The sound of the tracks inside the car was thumping louder all the time. "'Cause if you are, it was a stupid thing to do. You just about ended up under the wheels of this car."

He finally thought what to say. "Does this train go to California?" he called out over the noise.

All three men laughed.

"What do you want in California?" the big guy, the one standing, asked.

"I hear there's work."

They laughed again.

"Don't know if they have child labor down there," the sitting man said, raising his voice but laughing at the same time.

"I'm older than I look," Jay said.

"What are you, an Indian kid?"

"No."

For a time there was nothing but the noise and the vibration of the floor against his back. What if everyone said he was a kid, and no one would give him a job? Maybe he should jump off now and walk back to Delta. But this still seemed better.

"This train goes on down to Milford, and it might be going on to California. But I got a feeling you're running away from your momma and she's crying already. This ain't no way for a kid to be bummin' around. You from Delta?" said the sitting man.

"No."

"I'll bet you are."

"I'm not. I came down from Salt Lake. I've been riding the rails for a while, working where I can. I'm not a kid. Not like you think. I'm a ballplayer. I want to catch on with a team in California."

But this brought the biggest laugh yet. The big man moved back to the side of the car and sat down not far from the others. "You gotta git better at lyin' if you want to run away. That's for sure."

Jay sat up, then slid back against the side of the car, on the opposite side from the big man.

"How long does it take to get to Milford?"

"I don't know," the big man said. "I ain't never been this way before. I just asked a guy and that's what he said. It's going to Milford. That's still in Utah, I think."

Jay knew it was, but he didn't say so. He decided not to say anything. But he knew Milford wasn't very far, and maybe at that point he'd have to get some help from these guys, to know how to switch trains or whatever he had to do. He needed to get them on his side so they would help him. He thought about Gordy, the way he'd do it. Even Ken.

"I've had a lot of trouble," Jay said, and then realized he hadn't said it loud enough. He raised his voice, said it again, and then added, "My old man beats up on me, and my mother doesn't care. She just lets him do it. I gotta get somewhere else where I can make my own way."

But the words had cost him. They had more truth in them than he liked, and they were words he had never said before. Mom never had stopped his dad, and sometimes he'd hated her for that. He wiped the sweat from his face, pushed his hair back, and knew for the first time that he'd lost his hat, maybe back there when he'd fallen.

The second man who'd spoken to him was thin-faced, with a narrow nose and skinny arms sticking out from an old shirt rolled up above his elbows. "That ain't much different from a lot of guys on these trains. I left home at sixteen." He pushed his own hair back from falling in his eyes. "But you ain't no sixteen."

"I soon will be. I'm fifteen now."

"Or maybe thirteen."

"No. I'm just small for my age."

"You really from Salt Lake, or where?"

"I've lived lots of different places. But I've played a lot of ball. I might not hook up with a team right away, but teams are looking for players now, with so many away in the war. If I can work a while and keep practicing, I can maybe make a semipro team. I wanna play in the majors someday."

"The best thing you could do is go to high school, get yourself some education."

"Maybe I can do that. You know, in California."

"Soon as you try, they'll want an address, your dad's signature, and all that kind of stuff. I know all about that."

But Jay didn't really think he'd stay in school, no matter what his mother always said to him. He could go to a store, or maybe a factory, and tell the manager that he needed to work to help his mother while his dad was in the service, and then claim he went to school, too. Something like that. If he got some work at a grocery store, he could maybe get enough to eat. In California it was warm all the time. He could figure out a place to live and some way to practice baseball. He'd need to get himself another glove. The old one his dad had bought him was just a cheap one anyway. To be a really good player, he needed a better one.

The trouble was, he was making up a story and he knew it. He didn't know if any of this could really work out the way he was thinking it. But the train was real, and it was getting farther away from Delta every minute. His stomach felt sick when he told himself he was alone now and maybe always would be.

He thought of his mom, holding him when he was little, back in Salt Lake. "You have to mind your dad," she would say. "You know how mad he gets." He had hated her for that, still hated her sometimes. But she had been everything to him then. At least she'd cried when she'd seen his bruises, and he'd cried when he'd seen hers. She would cry today, once she knew he was gone. He thought again of jumping back off the train and heading home. But he knew what everyone would be saying about him.

And Ken was leaving. Nothing ever worked out right.

"I'll tell you what," the man with the thin face said. "If I had it to do over, I'd stay home. I left my family, and I ain't never been back, and I'm not even sure where they are now. I'd rather see my mother and my little brother than anything else in this world. If I can build up a few dollars working on the coast, then I'm going back to Indiana and figure out some way to find 'em."

"If you get a few dollars, you're going to get drunk, like every other time," the big man said. The third man, who hadn't said a word yet, laughed again. He was wearing bib overalls, farmer boots, and an old hat. It was just a floppy piece of felt with a hole worn all the way through at the front, where it had been gripped so many times.

"Go on. Jump off now, here where there's some sand," the big man said. "You can still walk back to Delta before the heat's too bad."

"What do I want with Delta?"

"That's where you're from. And I'll tell you how I know. This is the first train you ever jumped. You don't know how to do it. So don't tell me you've been riding around on trains. You don't have no gear, either, not like a guy who's been out on the road for a while. I'll tell you what else. You got in a fight with your old man, but he ain't half so bad as you think he is right now. You've been eatin' good, and that's more than you might be able to say pretty soon." When Jay didn't say anything, the man added, "And one more thing. You ain't going to convince no one that you're fifteen."

"Well, that's what I am, whether you think so or not."

They laughed again, all three of them, but this time he laughed with them. He needed to be friends with them.

"What's your name?" he asked, looking across the car.

The big man said, "Mac is what people call me."

"Where you from?"

"Nowhere now."

"He was in the war, out in the Pacific," the thin man said. "He got shot through both legs, so they mustered him out of the Marines. He went home and found his wife living with—"

"Hey! You don't need to tell the kid all that." He looked across at Jay. "I ain't like these two. I may take a drink now and then, but I ain't no wino. Jack here, he's feebleminded now, his brain all burnt up from drinking anything he can find with alcohol in it. I found him in Grand Junction, half-dead, and I've helped him a little since then. But it's what happens most of the time to the guys out here on these trains."

Mac looked over at the guy he'd called Jack. Jack was grinning, but Jay wasn't sure the guy even knew what anyone was talking about. "So jump now. Go back home."

"I can't. I can't go back. Will you help me get to California?"

"No."

"I will," the other fellow said, the one with the narrow face.

"What's your name?"

"Wayne."

"Okay, Wayne," said Jay. "We'll partner up for a while."

But that was one more reason to laugh, and maybe the reason to stop talking. The other men leaned back, let their eyes shut. He could see their bodies jiggle, their loose clothes shake. He realized they probably slept on the trains as much as they could.

He didn't shut his eyes. He watched the men, watched the open door, felt the heat rise inside as the rushing air kept getting hotter. But there was way too much to think about, and he didn't want to think. He just needed to keep moving ahead, doing whatever came next.

Maybe an hour went by, maybe twice that much—he couldn't be sure—but he realized that the clacking, the vibration, had begun to slow. "This must be Milford coming up," said Mac, as though from his sleep.

Wayne said, "This is where the trouble usually comes. What's your name, boy?"

"Jay." He said it without thinking, and then wondered whether he should have.

"Okay. We can probably sit tight here. There's a chance we'll get rousted—and you never know what the railroad guards in some of these little towns will try to do to you. Some sheriff with nothing to do will toss you in jail, or a guard will beat on you, just because he wants to. If they find us and throw us off, don't say nothing to anyone. Just call everyone sir, and say you're down on your luck or something. You might have to say some of what you been tellin' us, whether it's lies or not. But if you can, stick with me and I'll think of something. I could say you're my boy, but I don't think they're going to buy that one."

"Best thing is to hand him over to the sheriff," Mac said. "They can send him home."

Wayne didn't answer. He said to Jay instead, "Move back into the dark a little more, and just don't say nothing while we're in the yard. Chances are, this here car is staying on this train and we'll get through here."

Jay nodded, and then he slid over, but he didn't want to be too close to any of these guys. He had the better part of a dollar in his pocket. His grandpa had paid him for his work a while back and made him save most of the money, but Grandpa had said he could keep a dollar spending money, and so far he had spent only fifteen cents. He wondered if Wayne wasn't hoping to get a little money off him—to buy something to drink.

The train slowly rolled to a stop. The heat in the boxcar got a lot worse as the air stopped moving. He heard someone talking, but far off, and he figured he was going to make it past Milford all right. Another few minutes passed before he heard footsteps crunching in the cinders next to the tracks, and then he heard a voice. "Anyone in there?"

The men were silent, but a man's head appeared and then his shoulders. He was standing on something, looking in. Jay held still, held his breath, but the man said, "All right, you guys. Outa there."

"We ain't bothering nothing," Wayne said. "We're just—"

"We're switching this car off, boys. I won't worry much if you find another car with a door open, but I ain't seen any. The company is telling us to shut everything up."

Wayne got up and whispered to Jay, "Wait until last. He might walk away before we're all off." Mac was helping Jack get to his feet, and then he walked him to the door. He got down first and helped Jack come after. Wayne jumped down next, and then Jay stepped to the door. But when he did, he saw the railroad guard, or whatever he was, standing nearby. He jumped down, but as soon as he hit the cinders, the man said, "Hey, boy, what do you think you're doing?"

"He's traveling with me," said Wayne. "He's my nephew. I promised his mother I'd get him down to California where his grandparents live."

He watched the man, saw the firmness go out of his face.

But Mac said, "That's a lie. This kid jumped on in

Delta. His name might be Jay. That's what he said it was. I'll bet if you call up there, you'll find out some kid's run off and they're already looking for him."

The guard shook his head. "How old are you, kid?"

"Fifteen. Almost sixteen."

"Yeah, sure." He took hold of his arm. "Come with me."

"Sorry, kid," said Mac. "But this way's better. I can promise you that."

More promises, he thought. Everyone made promises.

CHAPTER 14

JAY WAS SITTING IN THE SHERIFF'S OFFICE IN MILFORD. THE SHERIFF was hunched over his desk, leaning on his elbows, a sheet of paper in front of him. Jay could see how worn his shirt was. The cuffs and the collar had little threads hanging off them. He was not an old man, but his skin looked like leather, like he'd spent his whole life outside. "So first, just tell me, honest, what your name is."

Jay had thought about a name. "John Belnap," he said. He had known a kid in Salt Lake named Belnap.

"That guy you were caught with said your name was Jay."

"They call me that sometimes."

"So, John—or Jay—Belnap, where you from?"

"I just travel."

A little smile slowly made dents in the corners of

the sheriff's mouth. "That's about as true as you being 'almost sixteen.' You probably made up that name, too. Tell me what's going on. I know you got rousted off that train with those bums, but you're not hardened down. I figure that was your first train ride."

Jay glanced at a dusty old wooden clock on the wall. It was just after eleven o'clock. He wondered if his grandpa was looking for him by now. Maybe Ken had gone into town and told Grandpa that he'd run off. Jay needed to write a letter and tell everyone he was okay, so that everyone would stop worrying.

What he had to do before he thought about all the rest, though, was lie to this sheriff and then get away from Milford. "Nothing's going on. I just heard there was work in California, and I need work."

"One of those bums said you got on the train up by Delta."

"He's nothing but a wino. He doesn't know where I got on."

"So where *did* you get on?"

"Salt Lake. But I'm not from there."

"Right. You're from all over the place. You ride the rails." The sheriff let his head sag almost onto his chest, and then he shook it slowly back and forth. "I don't need this on a Friday. You know that?" He leaned back in his upholstered desk chair, the cover on it as worn as his shirt. "I told my wife this morning I was going to drive her down to Cedar City to do some shopping. I don't much like doing that, but it's sure better than having to figure out what to do with you."

"I can just move on."

"Yeah, sure. And catch another train? You're lucky those hoboes didn't knock you over the head and take everything you've got on you—like that wristwatch you're wearing. If you were just a little bigger, they probably would have."

"They were nice fellows. I've met a lot worse."

The sheriff was thinking things over. He seemed like a pretty good guy. That was the trouble; he was too good to just send Jay on his way.

"You look like you could be Navajo. You didn't come off the reservation, did you?"

"No."

"I guess not. Not dressed the way you are. My guess is, that bum was right—you came out of Delta. I'm going to get in touch with the sheriff up there and see if some kid has taken off. But you could save me a bunch of trouble. If that's what it is—you got mad at your old man and ran off this morning—you might as well tell me. I'm going to find out anyway."

"Are you going to put me in jail?"

The sheriff let out a gust of breath. "Sure I am. You were breaking the law—jumping on a train like that. But if you tell me where you're from, we'll let that go. I'll get you home and that'll be the end of it."

Jay didn't believe that. The guy was too nice to stick him in jail. He wondered, though, if he called the sheriff in Delta, what would anyone know? The sheriff might not know he was missing. And he might not know that Kimball Reid's grandson's name was Jay.

"I've got a better idea," Jay said. "Give me a ride over to Cedar City when you take your wife shopping. I can hitchhike from there. I'll just move on and you won't have to worry about me."

The sheriff grinned. "Don't think I wouldn't like to do just that," he said. "I'd like to give you five dollars and put you on a bus—just to get you out of my life."

"That would be all right too," Jay said, and smiled at the man.

But the sheriff was thinking again. He sat for a time, looking past Jay toward the back wall, and then he finally said, "What I'm going to do is walk you over to the Star Café. I'll leave you with one of the waitresses over there. I don't like to do it, but I think I might have to handcuff you to a table, just so you won't take off again. You're not my only problem this morning. I got a few other things I need to take care of. Then I'll make that call up to Delta."

"That's a waste of your time. I'm not from there. I told you that."

"That might be right. But it's the only lead I have. The trouble is, if you just took off this morning, it could be no one's even figured out you're gone. The sheriff might have to check around and then call me back. But I can't leave you at the café forever. I will stick you in that cell back there if you don't give me any options. So do you want to come clean now?"

He almost did. But he thought of seeing everyone, and he just couldn't do it. "I told you I'm not from Delta."

"I know. But every time I start thinking you might be giving me the lowdown, I look at you and think, 'If he'd lie that much about his age, and do it with a straight face, he's probably lying about everything else.'"

"I just look younger than I am."

"Yeah, yeah. You told me that before." He stood up. "I'll bet you could use something to eat about now."

Jay nodded.

"Okay. I'll buy you something over there, and then I won't feel so bad about all this. I just keep thinking how I'd feel if it was my kid run off—and I'll tell you, I got a couple of sons who just might get something like that into their heads someday." He stood up. "Come on, walk over there with me. And if you'll promise me square that you won't take off, I won't put any cuffs on you."

He didn't answer. He didn't want to promise. But when they got to the café, the sheriff told him there was nowhere to run. And then he asked Jay again,

"Will you give your word? You won't make a run for it again?"

He nodded.

"Say it."

"I promise."

"Okay. You look to me like a boy who's been taught right. I'll trust you."

So the sheriff told the woman behind the counter—an Indian woman, he was pretty sure—to give him the twenty-five-cent lunch special, and he gave her thirty-five cents. "Jay here is going to stay an hour or two, and he's promised not to leave. I think he's run off from home somewheres and I'm trying to figure out where."

The woman nodded and slid the coins off the counter into the palm of her hand. She looked at him, studied him over, but didn't smile. He figured the dime was her pay for keeping an eye on him. It looked like he wasn't worth much.

"Thanks, Myrna," the sheriff said. "I got a lead on where he's from. I might have this figured out pretty fast."

He walked out, and Myrna took another look at Jay. "You Navajo?" she asked.

"Nope."

"I think so. At least some."

For some reason, he nodded. "Some," he admitted.

She nodded again, still looking at him intently. She

was a grown woman, but not very old—maybe in her twenties. She was kind of fat, especially in her cheeks. Her eyes looked out of little caves. Her voice was low, like a man's, but she sounded like she was worried about him. "I'll get you some lunch," she said, and walked back to the kitchen, through a tin door, one that swung back and forth.

Jay looked around. There were maybe a dozen people in the place, all of them bunched into booths. But no one was at the counter. He could walk out right now and no one would pay any attention. But where would he go? He didn't dare head for the railroad again, and towns were spread out. He could maybe hide somewhere along a ditch bank and then try to catch a train again that night. But he wanted to eat first.

The place smelled good—like coffee. His mom had always drunk coffee with his dad, even though Mormons weren't supposed to drink it. He liked the smell of it, but not the taste. There was a jukebox by the front door. It was playing "My Blue Heaven." He didn't like that song. His dad had always liked to sing it in the car when it came on the radio. He would try to make his voice deep and smooth, but he wasn't a good singer. "Just Molly and me and baby makes three," he would sing, like he and Jay and Mom were really happy, but he would sing it maybe the day after he had slugged Jay with the back of his hand and knocked him down.

Myrna came back with a hamburger and potato chips and a glass of milk. "Does that look all right?" she asked.

"Sure."

"That beef might be a little tough. It's hard to get good beef these days."

"I know." He picked up the hamburger and bit into it. It was sort of chewy, but it tasted good.

"You want ketchup?"

He nodded, and she found a bottle of ketchup behind the counter. But she stayed close and watched him, and that made him feel funny. "Do you like working here?" he asked, just to say something. He was still thinking he might take off. First, though, he had to get her thinking that he wasn't like that.

"No. I guess I don't," she said.

"How come you do it, then?"

She rubbed her hand along her forearm, then held it by her elbow, with her fingers pressing into her soft flesh. She looked sad. "I married a man from here," she said. "He's in the army now. At Fort Ord, in California. He's going to be gone for a long time."

"Do you have any kids?"

"Two. One's a baby girl, just two months old."

"Who takes care of her when you work?"

"The other woman who works here. We work shifts and trade off our kids."

"That works out okay, I guess."

Myrna nodded, but she still looked sad, like maybe she was thinking how bad it really was. "You should go home," she said. "It's not good to run off. You'll miss your family."

He thought about telling some more lies, but he didn't want to. Instead, he said something that was sort of true. "My dad's in the service."

"Where?"

He was chewing another bite of his hamburger. He thought he would tell her that his dad was a prisoner of war, and maybe that he was a hero. But he didn't want to do that anymore. "He died," he said instead. "His ship got sunk."

"Oh, Jay."

It felt better, in a way, to say it. But he didn't want her to feel bad. "He wasn't any good," he said. "He hit me sometimes. And he hit my mom. And he stepped out with other women."

"Was he Navajo?"

"Half."

"Things aren't good for Navajo men, Jay. It's not good how they live on the reservation. Too many of 'em drink. They don't know how to be Indians and they don't know how to be white—and your dad was some of both. He was probably a good man, deep inside."

"He played catch with me sometimes. A couple of times, anyway."

"See."

He tried the potato chips. They were sort of stale, but he didn't care. He was hungry.

"You're like me, Jay. You're not anything now."

He looked up. He didn't like the sound of that.

"I left the reservation to get a job, and I married a white man. Now I don't know what I am. I know everyone around here, and they like me okay. But I'm just an Indian to them. So I'm alone all the time."

"You have your kids."

"I know. And my husband loves me. He don't even care if I'm fat. He writes to me twice a week, sometimes more. He tells me in every letter that he loves me."

Jay didn't like what he was feeling—sorry for her, and for himself. He bit into his hamburger again.

"You need your mama, Jay."

"I know."

She waited until he looked up at her. "You need to go home."

"I can't."

"Why not?"

He didn't answer. He couldn't tell her that people had seen him dancing with a Jap.

"Whatever it is, it don't matter. Not so much as you think. You need to be with your mother. She already lost your dad—and it hurts her, even if he did those things."

"I think she wants to marry a guy she knows."

"That's all right." She reached toward him, patted his arm—like she wanted to start making promises. "Maybe he'll be nice to you."

He shrugged.

"I wish I had my people, Jay. I love my husband, and I love my children, but all my people are over on the reservation, and I never see 'em. It don't matter if you're Indian, or white, or anything else. You need to have your own people, whoever they are."

"I want to be a baseball player and make a lot of money."

"Everyone's going to be a ballplayer. Every boy in this country. You can't all be ballplayers."

He had been thinking that all day, but he kept trying not to. "I've got to figure something out, though. Something."

"Go back to your mama. She loves you."

He felt tears coming, but he fought them back. His mom did love him—he knew that—but she hadn't stopped Dad. Why hadn't she made him stop? It was what he thought about more than anything, but he tried not to. "It's like you said. I'm not anything." He didn't say it, but he was thinking about Dad's word: *worthless*.

"It don't matter. When I get my husband back, I'll be happy. It's the same for you. You've got a mama. But you've got nothin' at all if you run away." She patted him on the arm again.

But he could see it in her eyes. She didn't like being no one. He didn't either.

Myrna went off to the booths to pick up plates, to ask the people what else they wanted. He listened to all that, sat still, and forgot to eat. He was back to where he had started. There was nowhere for him to go. He did have his mother, but he was seeing everything clearer now. She hadn't looked out for him when he'd needed her.

Myrna came back in a minute and reminded him to eat, so he did. Then he said, "Myrna, I'm going to leave now."

"What do you mean? Run off?"

"Yes."

"You promised the sheriff you wouldn't do that."

"I know."

"Were you just lying to him?"

He hadn't been. Not at the time. But that wasn't what he said. "Everyone lies."

"Not everyone."

"They make promises and they don't keep 'em."

"Not always."

Jay got off the stool. "Thanks for lunch," he said, and then reached in his pocket and pulled out his change. He put another quarter on the counter.

She pushed the quarter back to him, but he didn't take it. "You weren't taught to tell lies, Jay. You were taught to be better than that."

He didn't know what he'd been taught. He turned and walked to the door. He stopped there, but he didn't look back at her. He tried to think what was right, and he couldn't think of anything. He stood looking through the glass door, watching a man walk by outside—a man holding himself tall, like maybe he was a soldier.

"Don't run off," said Myrna. But he could tell by her voice that she was still behind the counter, not coming after him. "You promised."

He reached for the doorknob, but his hand stopped. He stood again, not thinking about it too much, but knowing he couldn't go out. He stood there anyway. All he could think was that every choice he had was a bad one.

"Come back and keep me company for a while. I'll get you a piece of pie."

He turned around and walked back to the counter. But it wasn't for the pie.

Myrna was standing in the same place. She nodded to him. "I didn't think you would go," she said.

He slid the quarter to her again. She slid it back.

He sat down at the counter, but he didn't say anything. Myrna brought him some apple pie, and she went on about her work. But sometimes they talked, too, and she told him about growing up on the reservation. After a while the sheriff came back. "Well, Jay," he said, "my hunch was right. The sheriff up there in

Delta knew who you were. He said your grandpa had stopped by to let him know you were missing. Jay Thacker is your name, isn't it?"

"Yes."

"Your grandpa's driving down to get you. Will you stick around here with Myrna until he gets here? I don't want to hog-tie you to this stool or nothing like that."

Jay nodded. He wanted to stay a long time. He liked the smell of this place, and he liked Myrna. He liked that it was just waiting. Everything would change once Grandpa got here.

"Do you promise?"

"Yes." He looked over at Myrna.

"That's good. Everything will be okay now," she said.

He didn't think so.

"Do you live with your grandpa?" Myrna asked, after the sheriff was gone.

"Yes."

"What kind of work does he do?" She was pressing her fingers into her arm again, grasping tight, like she needed to hang on to something.

"He has a drugstore. And he's a patriarch."

"What's that?"

"He gives people blessings. It's something in our church."

Myrna nodded. "He's a holy man. That's what Navajos would call him."

Jay didn't think anyone ever called Grandpa that, but maybe that's what he was.

"I told you, Jay. You're a good boy. You've been taught right."

He didn't know if he was good or not.

"You keep your promises, Jay. That's the kind of boy you are. It's good to find that out about yourself."

CHAPTER 15

JAY SAT IN THE STAR CAFÉ FOR MORE THAN TWO HOURS. SOMETIMES he talked to Myrna. She knew some people in his family—not his grandma, but one of Jay's uncles. Jay had heard of him—his father's brother—but he didn't think he'd ever met him. He liked it, though, that she knew some of his people. She said that his uncle was in the war too, in the Marines. She said that lots of Navajos were in the Marines. They used their language to tell secrets and trick Japanese soldiers who tried to listen. They were heroes.

"You come from good people," Myrna said. "Chiefs and wise men. All the way back from before the white people came."

He thought about that while he waited. Grandpa Reid was a great man too, like a chief. A holy man. Maybe he could be like that, and like his uncle. Maybe he could play baseball, but if he couldn't, he could do something else. He did okay in school, at math and reading and everything else. His mother always told him he was smart. Maybe he could have a store of his own, like Grandpa. And maybe people would say that he was the best man in the whole town. Maybe he could bless people.

But he would have to leave Delta and try some other place.

When he got back, he would stay home, or go out to the farm after Ken was gone, and he wouldn't play ball with the boys. He wouldn't go to the drugstore or to church, and he wouldn't talk to anyone. When school started, he would sit at his desk and do his work, and then he would go home right after. He'd do that as long as he had to, and then he would go to college maybe, and study how to run a store or something like that. And he could still practice baseball alone.

Most of the people left the café after they had lunch. Myrna stood by him, but she didn't always talk. She liked him, though; he could tell that. He told her a few more things. He finally told her about Ken and how he had shown Jay how to dance.

"That don't matter," she said. "Indian men do dances—all of them together, with no women. It's not wrong to do that."

Myrna didn't understand about Lester and the things he had said. There was no way to explain it to her.

"Look at me, Jay," she told him. "A heart is good or not good." She pushed her finger against her chest. "And you have a good heart. If people know you, they'll like you all right. Don't worry about other things."

Jay liked hearing all that, but Myrna hadn't seen those boys at the dance, the way they had looked at him.

It was the middle of the afternoon when Grandpa finally walked into the café. Jay saw him in the mirror behind the counter, but he didn't turn around. He just waited to hear what he'd say. Grandpa came up behind him and patted his back. "Come on, Jay," he said in a soft voice. "Let's go home."

He got off the stool and turned around. He looked up at his grandpa to see how his face looked. He didn't look mad. He looked a little sad, maybe.

"Did they feed you something here?"

"Yes."

Grandpa looked at Myrna. "How much do I owe you, ma'am?" he asked.

"Nothing. The sheriff paid for it."

"Let me give you something," Grandpa said. "You can pay back the sheriff and keep a little tip for yourself."

"No. He don't want it. I don't either." The quarter was still on the counter. She pushed it at Jay again.

Grandpa had his wallet out, but he nodded. Jay

watched his eyes. Grandpa understood something. Maybe about Jay and Myrna being Navajos. So he picked up Jay's quarter and told Myrna, "Thank you."

Grandpa put his hand on Jay's shoulder. He felt the warmth of Grandpa's palm. "Let's go, son," he said. "You scared your mom half to death this morning— you scared all of us. We had people out in the desert searching for you."

Jay didn't like to think about that. It was one more thing people would be saying. But Grandpa's voice didn't sound angry. He had wondered what Grandpa would say when he got there, or in the car going back—whether he'd tell Jay he was worthless. But it was in Grandpa's face—he didn't feel that way.

So he said good-bye to Myrna, and she nodded to him, and then he walked out and got into the hot car, sat in the front with Grandpa. They rolled down the windows so the wind made lots of noise, and Grandpa drove north, but not fast, not angry the way Jay's dad had driven sometimes.

"You gave us a big scare," Grandpa said. "We thought you'd gotten lost in the desert or maybe got yourself bitten by a rattler, or something like that. I've never seen your mom so upset."

"Is she mad at me?"

"Mad?" Grandpa looked over at Jay. He looked surprised, his eyebrows both raised high. But then he laughed. "She might be a little by the time I get you home, but she's been crying an awful lot, and she had us all get down on our knees a few times to pray for you."

He wondered. Mom fussed about things, but he wondered what she would have done if he'd written her a letter and said he was okay, not to worry. Maybe she would have married Hal and figured she was better off.

"We know what happened at the dance, Jay. About Lester Callister saying you were out at the farm dancing with Ken. Is that what got you thinking you didn't want to stay around Delta?"

"I guess so. Mostly."

"Well, I can understand how that made you feel. But those things aren't so bad as you think. Most people won't give it a thought for more than a day or two."

"Gordy and the other boys will."

"Well, I don't know about that. Gordy and Ken went out together looking for you this morning. Ken came into town and told us what happened, about you running off the farm. He said he'd done some looking for a while but didn't know the country. I got hold of Gordy, since he knows that land about as well as anyone, and I sent them out looking for you."

"Gordy and Ken?"

"Yup. And Gordy recruited some of your other

friends. You know Gordy. He was talking all excited about forming up a 'search team' and all that—like he was going to be the star of a movie—and I said, 'Fine, but take Ken with you. You need someone older out there with you, and Ken wants to help.' I thought he wouldn't like that, but he seems to think Ken's quite the fellow—I guess because he plays ball so well."

"Yeah, that's right. He wants Ken to teach him, so he can make it to the major leagues."

Grandpa smiled, still looking straight ahead, holding the steering wheel with both hands. "That sounds like something Gordy would get into his head."

"Is Ken mad at me?"

"Well, you know how these things are. He told me he said some things when he was angry, and then ten minutes later he knew he shouldn't have. When I told Ken what happened at the dance, I could see how bad he felt. He wanted to find you more than anyone did."

"Ken's joining the army."

"I know. But you've known that all along, haven't you?"

"I guess." But Jay hadn't known, really—or hadn't thought about it much. Not until this morning. "He thinks he's going to be a hero, but he'll probably get himself killed."

Grandpa glanced over at him. "Is that one of the things you're worrying about?"

"I don't know. I guess." But he hadn't known he was worried about it—not until Grandpa had asked.

"Well, I know what you mean." Grandpa let one elbow rest in the window of the old Buick, like he was starting to relax a little more. Wind was blowing his shirt, making his sleeve puff out. His white hair was blowing too. "It's what we all worry about, Jay. We send these boys off, and we worry about all of them. It's the worst thing anyone ever thought up, these wars we keep fighting."

"Gordy wants to go to war. All the boys do."

"Of course they do. They hear all this hero stuff, and they all think it's a grand adventure. But the first time bullets fly, they learn fast. Ol' Gordy'll flatten himself out like a pancake once some shrapnel is flying around. Ken will too."

"He wants to win medals, so people will like him and everything. And give him a good job."

"I understand that, Jay. It's what we've forced these Japanese boys to feel—that they have to prove themselves. But I'll tell you what. It's a sad way to go about it. What God wants is for us to *stop* shooting each other. That's what I hope for you, that you never have to go to war."

Jay thought about all that. He let the wind blow on him and fill up his ears with the noise, and he tried to think of Ken keeping low, not getting himself shot. Maybe he wouldn't die. And he thought of Ken and

Gordy together, searching in the desert all morning. He wished now that he'd never told Ken that Japs were chickens and they would all get sent back to Japan.

"That little Gleed girl. Elaine. She came over and asked about you too. I guess the word got around town pretty fast this morning that you were missing. It had to, once Gordy got telling everyone."

"She came to our house?"

"She sure did. That's a cute girl, I'll tell you. And good as gold. She had a couple of the other girls from town with her, and they were all teary-eyed about you being dead out in the desert. Girls love a good drama, no matter what. I think Elaine has a little crush on you, though. You're a handsome boy, Jay. Girls are always going to pay attention to you."

"But what about me dancing with Ken? Did she say anything about that?"

"Not to me, she didn't. I think you made too much of that, son. Ken told people about how he was just teaching you some dance steps. People understand something like that."

Now Jay had a bunch more to think about. But he knew better than to let himself get too hopeful. He'd learned all his life that just when things started to look pretty good, they always took a turn back the other way.

Grandpa let a lot of time go by after that. Jay

watched the blacktop road as it rose and fell over little ridges, rolling out ahead through the sagebrush and junipers, the red-rock cliffs showing here and there. He wanted to talk to Grandpa, maybe ask him something, but he couldn't think of anything to say.

Finally Grandpa said, "You haven't said how you feel about going home. Do you wish we hadn't caught up with you?"

"No."

"Where were you going?"

"California."

"Just like all the kids around here. It's always California. What did you think you would do out there?"

"Work, I guess. And maybe be a baseball player."

Grandpa smiled a little, probably thinking that it was a silly idea—and one he'd gotten from Gordy. "All this because of this business about dancing with Ken!"

"Mostly."

"What else?"

"Because of Mom maybe wanting to marry that Hal guy."

"Well, see, that's just what I thought. You got a lot of stuff piled on top of you, all at once. That's more than one boy ought to have to carry. I can see where you thought you needed to make a break for it. But didn't you know you're too young to go off on your own?"

"I thought I wasn't."

"So what do you think now?"

"I don't know."

Grandpa took a longer look at him, then looked back at the road. "You're not going to run off again, are you?"

"No."

"Why not?"

"I was scared the whole time I was gone."

"Well, it's good you learned that." Grandpa drove for some time, watching ahead, but after a time he said, "Jay, I thought about a lot of things this morning. For one thing, you've been down here quite a while now, and I haven't taken you fishing or anything like that—the things I did with my own boys. I should have been a little bit more of a father to you. It's a hard thing for a boy not to have his father around. A lot of boys are facing that right now, but most of them aren't left in limbo, not knowing one way or the other about their dads being alive." Jay looked over at Grandpa, but he didn't know what to say. "Would you like to go fishing some time?"

"I guess so. I haven't gone for a long time."

"Well, we'll go. And I know some good places. Maybe we'll camp out one night, over by Fish Lake or somewhere like that. We'll catch us a mess of trout and eat 'em for breakfast, cooked over an open fire. You ever tasted anything like that?"

"No."

"Well, there's nothing better, and we're going to do it. I'll tell you something else. I was a heck of a ballplayer when I was a boy. I think you've got some of that in you, too. I can't get out and run as fast as I used to, and I can't pitch like I did at one time, but I know the grips and the motions. I can teach you plenty about throwing a curveball or a fastball that rises and makes a guy swing too low. Would you like to learn some things like that?"

Jay was smiling, just to think Grandpa knew that kind of stuff. "Sure."

Grandpa reached over and patted him on the shoulder, then left his hand there for a while. Jay thought of his dad, how he never did anything like that.

"I want to tell you something else," Grandpa said. "If you run away, it's like telling everyone you did something wrong. And you didn't. So here's what I want you to do."

Jay waited. He did need to know.

"You look people in the eye. That's one thing you can learn from Ken. People call him a Jap and maybe don't like to see him around town, but he looks people straight on, says hello all the same. You don't see him looking ashamed of himself."

"I know. That's what he said I should do too."

"And he's right. Maybe you're part Indian, and

maybe some people think that means something. And maybe that Callister kid made fun of you. But people like him only win if you let 'em. You look people in the eye and don't hang your head. You'll be just fine."

"Okay." Jay nodded and told himself that was right. It's what he would do.

"And don't run away. That was the most foolish thing you could have done. If you'd made it to California, do you think that would've done any good?"

"I guess not."

"Will you promise me never to do that again?"

"Yes. I promise." He thought of Myrna.

CHAPTER 16

WHEN JAY AND GRANDPA GOT HOME, GRANDMA WAS IN THE KITCHEN, fixing dinner. She said that Jay's mom had gone to work once she'd found out Jay was all right. He was glad, in a way, that she wasn't there—and maybe mad at him. He was hoping to go off to his room, since he didn't really want to see anyone. He knew Grandpa was right, that he had to look everyone in the eye, but he was scared to get started.

"I decided to cook my Sunday roast today," Grandma told him. "With lots of potatoes and gravy, because I know you like that. But maybe I should have fixed you bread and water, and maybe I should give you a darned good spanking. We were awfully worried about you, Jay." She was stirring the gravy, but she put her spoon down and walked to him. Then she pulled him to her and held him tight for a long time. "Don't ever scare us like that again. Okay?"

"Okay."

"Were you mad at us?"

"No. I just . . ." But Jay had no idea what to tell her.

"It never does any good to run away from things. Do you know that?"

"Yeah. Grandpa already told me that."

"Do you believe him?"

"Yeah."

He was glad she didn't ask any more questions. He got away and went to his room. He was dead tired, and dirty from falling down in the desert and riding on the train. He wanted to take a bath.

But he had no more than pulled off his boots when Grandma called down the hall, "Jay, there's someone here to see you."

He thought about yelling to her that he was already in the tub, but she knew that wasn't true. He walked down the hall in his stocking feet and saw Gordy standing just inside the front door. Ken was right behind him.

"Hey, Chief," Gordy called out, "welcome home. Glad to know you're not dead and eaten up by coyotes." He laughed, making that sound like rocks were in his throat.

Jay didn't want to smile, but he did.

"Me and Ken looked for you all morning. We tried to track you. We even found your hat. I told Ken your footprints stopped at the train tracks and you must've jumped a train. He didn't believe me. But what does he know? He grew up in California. He doesn't know one thing about the desert."

"I only know about important things," said Ken, but he wasn't laughing as much as Gordy was.

"Hey, guess what?" Gordy said.

But Grandma was calling, "Hey, boys, you don't have to stand there in the hall. Sit down in the living room."

"I'm too dirty," Jay said.

"Well, come in here, then."

So they walked into the kitchen and sat at the table, Ken and Gordy on one side and him on the other.

"I'll get you some grape juice," Grandma said, and she headed toward the cellar door.

"Guess what I'm going to do?" said Gordy. "After the war, I'm going out to San Francisco. Ken's going to show me the Golden Gate Bridge and all that other stuff. I'm going to learn how to be *cool*, too, like Ken." He let his head bob slowly up and down a couple of times, like maybe he thought that was part of being cool.

Jay knew Gordy liked learning baseball from Ken, but he hadn't thought they'd ever get to be friends.

"Cool maybe," Ken said, "but never as cool as me." But then his face started to look more serious, and he said, "Sorry about those things I said this morning, Jay."

Jay looked at the table. "I was the one who said all the bad stuff. I was mad."

"I know. I know about everything that happened."

"Hey, guess what?" Gordy said. "When we were out there looking for you this morning and couldn't figure out where you'd gone, we got talking about how you danced with Elaine, and how she was getting all sweet on you and everything, so Ken showed me how to jitterbug. I'm getting pretty good. I'm going to win Elaine back, next dance."

Ken was laughing now. He gave Gordy a little push on the shoulder. "You're not *that* good," he said.

"Did you know Ken's going in the army?" Gordy said. "He'll be killing Krauts before the year's out."

"I know," Jay said.

"Soon as I can, that's what I'm going to do too," Gordy went on. "Maybe we could go together, if the war lasts long enough—and kill Krauts together."

Jay noticed that Gordy didn't say he wanted to kill Japs, the way he usually did.

Jay had been thinking about the things Grandpa had told him—about being scared and getting flat on the ground when bullets started flying. He'd remembered about shooting birds and horny toads, and not liking to kill things. He didn't think he wanted to go to war. But he didn't say that.

"Then after the war, we'll play more ball and make it to the majors, like we talked about. Oh, and hey, we're going to play that ball game out at the camp next week. That's for sure now. I was worried this morning you wouldn't get back, and we wouldn't have a chance without you." Gordy laughed again, hard, and slapped the table. "That was one of the bad things about you gettin' yourself eaten up by coyotes."

Ken played like he was knocking Gordy over the head. "Nice way to talk," he said.

"You're going to play, aren't you?" Gordy asked Jay.

"I guess so." But Jay wasn't sure. He didn't know what the other boys were thinking about him. They weren't like Gordy.

"Ken says his boys can beat us, and he might be right—'cause we got some boneheads on our team— but we'll go down fighting, won't we?"

Jay looked at Ken. "How soon are you leaving for the army?"

"I don't know exactly. I'll sign up on my birthday, and then I have to go up to Salt Lake to be processed. It'll be a month or so before I leave."

Grandma was back with the grape juice. She said, "Is one of you boys strong enough to open this bottle?"

Ken stood up and reached for the bottle, and he twisted the lid off, easy. But Jay was still thinking that Ken would be gone soon, and maybe he was going to try too hard to be a hero. "Are you going to work on the farm until you go?" Jay asked.

"Probably so. I don't have anything better to do."

Jay was glad to hear that.

Grandma was pouring the grape juice. "You boys rest a little here for a minute and drink this juice. Then why don't you stay and have dinner with us?"

"You don't have to ask me twice," said Gordy. "Whatever you're cooking sure smells good."

"Maybe I better not," Ken said.

But Grandma said, "I know what you're thinking. But don't worry about it. You're always welcome with us."

"All right, then. I know you're the best cook in Delta. *Everyone* says that."

"More blarney," she said. She patted his cheek, almost like he was her grandson too. "Jay, you better get into the tub now, before dinner."

He agreed, but as he got up to leave, Gordy said, "Hey, Jay, did you really jump a train?"

"Yeah."

"How come you got off in Milford?"

"We got kicked off."

"What do you mean, 'we'?"

"Some guys were riding in the boxcar. I didn't know it until I got on."

"What? Hoboes?"

"Sort of. They were guys going to California to get work. One was a drunk. Maybe all of 'em were."

"Oh, man, I wish I'd gone with you. Why don't we do it together one of these days before school starts?

We could jump a train, ride down to Milford, then jump another one and ride back."

Jay was looking at his grandma, who was shaking her head, looking serious. "I almost didn't make it on. I jumped, and I didn't get all the way in, and one of those guys had to pull me on. I might've gone under the train wheels if he hadn't grabbed my arm."

Now Grandma was looking about ready to pass out, and Gordy was grinning wide. "Hey, man, you gotta tell us *everything*. Nobody around here ever did anything like that. You'll be famous."

"What about all the boys on the team? What are they saying about me?" Jay asked.

"You mean about dancing with Ken?"

Jay nodded.

"I just told 'em to shut their mouths. And they did. It's just one guy showing another guy something—like a coach teaching baseball, or something like that."

That didn't sound so bad. "Thanks," he said to Gordy.

But Gordy just shrugged, like he didn't know what Jay was talking about.

Later, everyone ate dinner. Mom came home, and she ate with them. She even talked to Ken some. Maybe she wanted to show Ken that she didn't mind doing that—since he'd looked for Jay and everything.

Gordy wanted to play baseball afterward, but Jay said he didn't want to. He just wanted to rest up.

He went down to his room after Ken and Gordy left, and he sat on his bed. He tried to think how he felt about everything now. After a while his mom came to his open door. "Hi," she said.

"Hi."

"How are you feeling?" She stopped in the doorway, the way she usually did.

"Tired, mostly."

"I guess you didn't feel like playing ball tonight."

"I'll play next week."

"Are you thinking like Gordy, that you want to play in the major leagues?"

"Sure. But every kid thinks that. Not many can make it."

Her voice was quiet tonight. She walked over and sat on the bed next to him. She had fixed her hair nice for dinner and put on lipstick, just like when Hal Duncan had been there.

"Some people think they have to be big shots to be happy. Baseball players, or something like that. But it's not that important. Look at Grandma and Grandpa, how happy they are."

"Grandpa's kind of a big shot."

Mom let out a little burst of air, a kind of laugh. "I guess," she said. "A big shot in Delta. But mostly he just loves every single person in town, so they all love him back."

"He blesses them too."

"Yes, he does. He puts his hands on their heads and pronounces blessings—but he does a lot of other things for people too." She slipped her arm around his shoulders.

"You said you got so you didn't like him when you were a kid."

"No, I didn't say that. I wanted to do whatever I had a mind to do, and he kept telling me I was making the wrong choices. I didn't like that, but I knew every second of every day that he loved me anyway. The same with my mom. It's why I could finally come home when things got bad for us."

"It's not too bad to be down here."

She tightened her grip on him, and when he looked at her, she was smiling. "That's not what you said last night."

"I know."

"This has been a hard summer for us, hasn't it?"

"You were worried a lot, I guess."

"Mostly I'm just impatient. I want to know for sure about your dad, one way or the other, and we just don't hear anything."

"Do you still think he could be alive somewhere?"

"No, I don't. But I miss him more than you might think. We love him, don't we?"

"Sometimes I hated him."

"I know. But let's love him now. Let's remember the best things."

"Okay." That was what Jay wanted to do. But he didn't want to cry, and he was starting to do that. His mom seemed to know, and she wrapped both arms around him.

"It might be a long wait before we know anything for sure," she said. "But that's just how things are. And it's what we have to accept."

"I know." He pulled back a little. He didn't want her to think he was being a baby about everything.

But she turned his chin so she could look at him. "Are you worried what people will say to you about Ken?"

"Yeah."

"What are you going to do about it?"

"Look 'em in the eye. That's what Grandpa said."

"He's right, too. It'll all blow over in a few days. I know it doesn't seem like it, but it will."

He looked toward the wall, away from his mom. "Some people don't like Indians."

"But we don't have to worry about 'some people,' do we?"

"I guess not."

"I'm sorry about the way I treated Ken. I guess I was being 'some people' myself."

Jay was glad she could think that way.

Mom got up and walked to the door, but then she turned around and leaned against the frame. "Jay, I'm sorry. I haven't been much of a mom to you this summer. I've spent too much time feeling sorry for myself."

Jay knew what she meant, but he didn't know what to tell her.

"I've had a lot of time to think today," she said. She looked away, like she was thinking again. She was wearing a summer dress, light as air, yellow with little white dots. She looked sad, though. "You're growing up now, Jay. I want to be honest with you from now on. For a long time I didn't want to say anything about your father because I knew how much you loved him. I wanted you to be proud of him."

"I used to hate him when he'd hit you. I wanted to hit him back, but I was too little." Jay felt his voice starting to shake, and he looked away again.

"I know. And I wanted to stop him when he would hurt you, but I was too scared of him."

He looked back at her. "Scared?"

"When he was mad, I never knew what he might do."

He hadn't thought of that—that she was scared too. "Why didn't you leave him? We could have moved down here."

Two tears slipped over the curve of her cheek-bones and slid slowly down her face. "I don't know, Jay. Every time I thought of it, I could only think of coming back here and admitting I'd been wrong all along. But I loved your dad too—even after he did all those things to us. He was always sorry after he hurt us, and he'd promise not to do it again. I wanted to believe him, so I stayed."

"You used to tell me that he was a good man, and I shouldn't hate him."

"I know. And it's still true. He could be so good. And he was funny and full of life. I still love him, Jay. Even if he's dead, I love him."

There was something Jay had always known he should tell her. "One night, when you were working, he brought a woman home with him. They were drunk, I think, and they were laughing, and he kept saying to be quiet so she wouldn't wake me up."

She slowly lowered her head. "I'm sorry," she said. "I didn't know you had to put up with something like that. And I didn't know how many times he'd gone out with other women until I started hearing things after he was in the navy. But that's another reason I should have left him."

"He's not coming back, though, is he?"

"No. He's not."

Jay tried to think how he felt about that, but it was Myrna who came to his mind. "I met a Navajo woman down in Milford. She knew Dad's family. She said he came from good people—chiefs and wise men."

"And that's how we're going to remember him. Maybe if he'd had another chance, he would have done better. That's what we'll always think, anyway."

Jay wanted to do that. But the thoughts never went away—the memories of the way he would yell and swear, and the things he would say. "He used to tell me I was worthless. I didn't even know what it meant, but I hated when he said that." Jay had been fighting not to cry, but now he bent forward, cupped his hands to his face, and finally couldn't hold back.

His mom came back to him and took him in her arms. "Don't remember that," she said. "When he was angry, he would say things that he didn't mean. He loved you, Jay. No matter what he ever said, just remember that. He loved you more than anyone."

Jay didn't know if it was true. But he was glad he had finally told her, and glad his mom was holding him.

"We're going to be okay, Jay. I'm going to stand up tall for once in my life, and I'm going to be more what I ought to be. I'm going to be a better mother to you."

"Are you going to marry Hal?"

Mom took hold of Jay's shoulders and held him away from her, so she could look into his face. "I don't know, Jay. I've told him that we're just friends for now—until I know for certain about your dad. But I would never marry him until you were okay with it."

"Is he a nice guy?"

"He is, Jay. I think you would like him. He likes to fish, and he likes baseball. He was a good ballplayer in high school, pretty much the best at every sport. Maybe he could coach your baseball team." She laughed. "I think you need someone besides Gordy."

Jay wasn't sure about that. He still didn't like to think about Hal coming to see his mom.

"Would it be all right if I ask him to help you guys?" his mom said.

"I guess." He didn't like the idea, but he told himself he had to do what Ken always said to do: make the best of the situation, whether he liked it or not.

CHAPTER 17

ON SUNDAY HAL CAME OVER TO THE HOUSE FOR DINNER. JAY DIDN'T talk to him much, but when he offered to help coach Jay's team, he said that would be okay. He figured Mom had said something to him or he never would have thought of the idea. But when they talked a little baseball, Hal seemed to know what he was talking about. He couldn't come over every night, he said, but he'd come as often as he could.

"You and Ken could coach us together until Ken leaves," Jay said. "He can't come every night either."

So that was how it was left. Hal would help coach, and he would go with them to the game next Saturday. Ken would be there too—but for that day, he would be coaching the other team.

On Monday Jay went back to work on the farm. He and Ken. They were still fixing fences, stretching wire and putting in new posts that had fallen down or broken off. Ken used the tractor to pull the wire some-times, and the two got a lot done. Toward the end of the day, they took a break and drank some water. Ken was sitting on the tractor. Jay was standing by the fence, his elbow hooked over a fence post.

"Are you excited to get out of here?" he asked Ken.

"Sort of. It's a good time for me to go. You're going back to school before too long, and I would have been out here all by myself. I would have hated that."

Jay nodded, but he didn't know how to say what he was thinking. So instead he asked, "Are you sort of scared about going into the army?"

Ken leaned forward with his arms resting on top of the steering wheel. He was wearing big leather gloves that looked almost like baseball gloves. "I've been thinking about that. I've been anxious to sign up for a long time. But now, with the time coming up fast, it's kind of different."

"What's so different?"

Ken looked over him, above his head. "I always say how brave I'll be, but maybe I won't be brave at all. I don't know if you can know that until the time comes."

"I'll bet you will be. You'll probably get a bunch of medals."

Ken didn't answer that.

"Grandpa said, when bullets start flying, everyone gets scared."

"That's what I've heard too. But I'd hate myself if I turned into a chicken."

"You won't."

"Maybe I won't be a hero, though."

"You don't have to be one, do you? Just being a good soldier is okay. You don't *have* to win medals."

"Guys like me have to. We have to prove ourselves."

"But it's stupid just to run out somewhere and get killed."

"I won't do that."

"It scares me that you will." Now it was Jay who couldn't look at Ken.

"You mean, get myself killed the way your dad did?"

"Yeah."

"I'll play it smart. Don't worry about that."

Jay pulled his gloves off and acted like it was important to take a good look at them.

"This has been a bad time for me, Jay. I hate living out at Topaz, and I hate having everyone stare at me in town. That's why I want an American uniform. People can stare if they want, but at least they'll know I'm fighting for us, not them."

"But don't take a bunch of chances."

"Okay. I'd rather not die, if you want to know the truth." Ken smiled. "How come you didn't mind working with me, Jay?"

"I don't know. It turned out you were just a regular guy."

"No, I'm not. I'm the coolest guy you ever met."

"Yeah." But when he said it, Jay felt tears coming, and he turned away. He pretended he needed to get some more water, and he walked back to the house.

Hal came to practice Monday night, and Ken came some of the nights that week too. The boys didn't get a whole lot better, but they learned a few things. They started running the bases better, and the outfielders learned which guy to throw the ball to after somebody got a hit.

On Saturday, Hal and Gordy's dad drove cars out to Topaz, so the boys didn't have to take the bus. Gordy's mom almost had a stroke about that, but Brother Linebaugh said he'd always wanted to take a look at the camp for himself.

Jay had heard all about Topaz, but he was surprised by what it was really like. The houses were long wooden buildings, like army barracks, with only tar paper on the outside. They sat in rows and in blocks, reaching way out a mile each way. Out beyond the wire fences there was nothing but desert, not one tree anywhere. He saw all the gray dirt, like powder, that Ken had told him about, even saw how it could blow when a breeze would kick up. He noticed, too, the way people had done their best to make things look nice: with greasewood cut to look like decorations and white rocks set out to line the walkways.

It was a sad-looking place, in a way, but the people didn't look down in the mouth. When the boys reached the baseball field, in the center of the camp, a lot of the people from the camp had come over to watch. There were teenagers in bunches, and lots of parents, some of them sitting on a little set of bleachers.

"Hey, look at that girl," Gordy said. "Wow. She's a knockout."

There was a girl in a black skirt, about knee length, with a sleeveless blouse. She had her hair in a ponytail. She *was* cute. So were a lot of the girls. Some of them were doing cheers, yelling that their team was going to win. It was sort of like going over to the high school in Delta—except for the dirt and the tar-paper barracks.

"Come with me for a second," Ken said to Jay. The two walked down a dirt street past maybe a dozen of the barracks, and then Ken turned in at one. He knocked on a door at one end, then opened the door and said, "Ma, are you here?"

Jay heard a high-pitched voice answer, but not in English. Ken walked in, and then held the door for Jay. He stepped into a little square room with a coal stove on one side and a bed on the other. There were blankets hanging up, making walls. There were two wooden chairs, and a box that looked liked it had been made from scrap lumber. It was a table, kind of, with shelves underneath. Everything was pushed together close, so there was hardly any room.

"This is Jay," Ken said in English to his mother. "The boy I work with."

The woman bowed from the waist. "So happy to meet you," she said, and now she sounded like Jay's mom or his grandma. She could speak English *and* Japanese. She was smiling, too, and her smile was like Ken's. She was dressed like Jay's mother, in a house-dress with little flowers on it, but her hair was more fancy, sort of wound up on her head.

He didn't know what to do. He bowed a little himself. "Nice to meet you," he said.

"Is Father going to the game?" she asked Ken.

"Yes."

One of the blankets moved, and a man stepped through. "Good morning," he said. "How are you?"

"This is Jay," said Ken.

Ken's father didn't bow. He reached out his hand. "Very nice to meet you," he said, and it sounded important, the way a mayor, or someone like that, might talk. But it sounded almost like Japanese, too—not as American as the way Ken spoke. "Would you like to sit down? I'm sorry we have so little room here."

"It's okay, Dad," Ken said. "We have to get over to the game. I just wanted Jay to meet you, and I wanted to be sure you were coming."

"Yes. I will come."

"Dad likes baseball," Ken told Jay. "He goes to a lot of the games."

His father smiled and bowed his head. "Yes," he said.

"Jay's a very good player," said Ken. "Very good. We work together at the farm, too."

"Yes," Ken's father said again.

"And he's my best friend—my very best friend."

Jay nodded. But he hadn't known that.

"After the war, we'll be friends again. I promised him I'll be careful and not get hurt. The same as I promised you." Ken put his hand on Jay's shoulder, left it there. And as they walked back toward the diamond, he still had his hand on Jay's shoulder. And he told him something. "I wanted you to see how we live—how things are in those barracks. I don't think many people in Delta know about that."

"It's crowded up, really bad."

"My two sisters sleep together behind some of those blankets, and my parents sleep behind the other ones. I sleep in that room you saw, when I'm there. The heat from the stove gets to me, but not to them. In the winter, they almost freeze."

"It doesn't seem right to crowd up people like that."

Ken stopped and looked at him. "It isn't right. Remember that—and maybe you could tell some people."

"Okay."

When the game started, Gordy pitched. Jay played shortstop. Hal was the coach, but Ken came over and said, "Hey, have a good game, you guys. Remember the stuff we've been teaching you."

But the game didn't start very well. The Delta boys—they'd decided to call themselves the Rabbits, because that was what they would all be at Delta High—were up first. The Topaz team had a pitcher who didn't look big enough to throw very hard, but it turned out he could fire a good fastball, and he had a curve, too.

The first two Rabbits struck out. Jay came up next. He let a couple of pitches go by, just to see if he could get ahead of the pitcher. The trouble was, both pitches got called strikes. Gordy was in the on-deck circle—or at least where one should have been. He yelled, after the second pitch, "Hey, ump, are you blind? Both those pitches almost hit the dirt."

People in the bleachers didn't yell back at him, but Jay heard some of them laugh, like they figured Gordy didn't know what he was talking about.

Jay swung at the third pitch and at least got some wood on it. He bounced a grounder toward the second baseman, who scooped it up like a pro and flipped it over to first before he was halfway down the baseline. That was the end of the first inning for the Rabbits.

Gordy took a pounding. He was trying to throw too hard, and he was throwing wild. He walked two batters, and then he started aiming his pitches, trying to throw strikes, and the Topaz guys started hitting shots all over the place. Jay made two good plays at shortstop, both on ground balls, or the inning might have gone on the rest of the day. When a guy finally hit a pop-up and Gordy waved everyone off and caught it himself, the inning was finally over, but the score was 8-0.

Gordy started out the next inning and acted like a big leaguer, knocking dirt off his shoes with his bat and spitting on his hands. But he swung three times and never touched the ball. It was three up, three down for the Rabbits again.

When Gordy walked back to the mound, he yelled to his teammates, "Come on, now. Let's show these guys we can play this game."

That caused more of the people in the crowd to laugh. Jay saw the people in the bleachers talking to one another and smiling. He could tell they didn't think much of the team from town. Hal was clapping and calling out, "Buckle down now, boys. Let's get some outs."

One thing Jay had learned, Hal did know a lot about baseball. He was kind of fun, too. He liked to make jokes and everything. Gordy liked him—even though Gordy still thought *he* was the boss of everyone.

The guy who played first base, quite a tall guy, was coming up to bat. "What are you grinning about?" Gordy yelled at him.

"At you. And that pitch you call a fastball."

Gordy didn't answer him. He turned away and looked toward Jay. "All right. Let's *show* these guys," he said.

Gordy turned around, stepped on the little board that was used for a pitching rubber, and let fly with a pitch that flew way over the catcher's head and all the way to the screen. Maybe that was a way of showing off his fastball, but it got another big laugh from all the Topaz players—and from the crowd, too. The next pitch was in the dirt.

"Come on, Gordy, just pitch to him," Jay yelled. It was probably the first time he'd ever tried to give Gordy any advice. But Gordy nodded, as if he knew already that was what he had to do. His next pitch wasn't so hard, and it was over the plate. The tall kid took a hard swing and topped the ball. It bounded toward Dwight, who was playing second. The ball looked easy enough to handle, and Dwight got himself in front of it. But then it took a crazy bounce, off to the left. Dwight stabbed across his body at the ball and got a little leather on it, but it bounced off his glove and rolled into right field. At least Will, out in right, hustled in, and he held the batter to a single.

"What's wrong with this field?" Gordy shouted to the umpire. "It's got rocks on it or something. How are we supposed to get anybody out if the ball bounces around like that?"

The umpire smiled a little, and some of the people

in the crowd gave Gordy a hard time. "We play on the same field," one of the players yelled. And someone in the bleachers called out, "Get some strikeouts—the way our pitcher does."

He thought that was fairly polite, and exactly what Gordy had coming, but ol' Gordy was fuming. He wound up and threw another pitch in the dirt. Lew was playing catcher. He managed to block the ball, so at least the guy at first didn't take second.

Gordy got the ball back, and he stared hard before he wound up. He took something off the next pitch, and the batter mistimed his swing. He scooted a little grounder off the end of his bat, straight back toward Gordy. Gordy probably should have taken the guy at first and gotten the sure out, but he spun around and looked toward second. Jay was already breaking to the bag. Gordy threw the ball for the force-out, and maybe threw too hard. The ball sailed, but Jay went up after it, caught it, and came down behind the bag. He lunged for the base, but the tall kid who had been on first was barreling in hard. He slid with his foot high, caught Jay in the chest, and sent him flying.

Jay landed on his side and rolled over in a puff of dirt, like smoke. His vision was swimming, maybe from the blow he'd taken, maybe from the dirt. He scrambled up as fast as he could, the ball still in his glove. But just as he got to his feet, he saw Gordy there, driving his fist into the tall kid's jaw, then rolling over on top of him. And then Gordy was scrambling back up and so was the Japanese player. He popped Gordy in the eye, and he went down again.

By then guys were coming from every direction. They grabbed one another, pushing and shouting, and more fists flew. Jay was wondering what to do when a fist caught him in the side of the head. He didn't go down, but he turned and took another punch that caught him in the neck. He grabbed the guy who had hit him, and the two tumbled onto the ground. He had the kid in a headlock and was squeezing with all his strength. About then, someone grabbed him and jerked him to his feet. It was Ken. "Stop it, Jay. Back away," he was saying.

He did back off, and by then the umpire and Hal were out there, pulling kids apart. It took a couple of minutes to get the two teams separated. Then they all stood back and glared at one another. "We're not going to have any more of this," Ken was yelling. "I'll call this game right now unless you're willing to step up and shake hands."

No one moved. Jay thought he wouldn't mind getting back in the car. He saw no reason to keep the game going. He glanced around and thought he could see that most of the guys on his team felt the same way. It was almost better to call off the game on account of a fight—and tell that story back in Delta.

Who wanted to admit that they got knocked all over the place on the field?

"Well, which is it?" Ken asked. "Are you going to shake hands and then play some ball, or are we calling the game off?"

He could see the tall kid who had slid with his foot in the air. He was looking down at the ground. Maybe he was ashamed. Gordy had his hands on his hips, but he didn't look so mad anymore. And then Jay saw him start to smile, and the smile turned into his big-teeth grin. "Hey, my eye is swelling shut. You got me good," he said.

The tall kid looked up, obviously surprised.

"That's the best fight I've ever been in—at least in a baseball game," Gordy went on.

He saw some of the Japanese kids start to smile.

"I fought a kid at school one time, but he punched like a girl. You guys can go after it. I gotta hand it to you."

The smiles were getting bigger.

"I'll tell you what. Let's play, and I'll pitch with one eye. But you better look out for my fastball now. I can't even see right."

"What fastball?" one of the kids said, and everyone laughed. Both teams. Even Ken and the umpire.

"Okay, here's what I'll do," said Gordy. "I'll let Chief pitch. He's got a good arm. Maybe he can get somebody out. But let's play ball."

So they all shook hands and went back to playing, and Jay pitched. He wasn't great, but as it turned out, he was better than Gordy. He even got a couple of strikeouts when the Topaz team started putting in their weaker players. He also got a hit off their second pitcher, a double down the left-field line, and then Gordy smacked a single up the middle and Jay scored the only run for the Rabbits. He didn't know what the score turned out to be, and he didn't want to know, but he was sure it was way more than twenty for the Topaz team and just that one for the Rabbits.

But after the game, the tall guy came over to him and said, "Ken told me to say I'm sorry. I shouldn't have slid into you like that."

Gordy was standing next to Jay. "That's what Ken told you to say, but what about you? What do *you* say?"

"I shouldn't have done it."

"It didn't hurt much," Jay said. "Not for long."

"You're the best player on your team. Especially when you play shortstop."

"That's probably right, Chief," said Gordy. "You played really good. I gotta work hard to get as good as you now." He looked back at the Japanese boy. "We want to make it to the majors."

"That's what I want to do too," the boy said.

"Just about everyone does," said Jay.

"What are you?" asked the boy.

"What?"

"Are you an Indian?"

"Not exactly."

"Is your name Chief?"

But Gordy answered for him. "No. It's Jay. He doesn't like to be called Chief. And he's not anything. He's just an American."

The tall kid nodded.

Ken was walking toward them by then. "I'll tell you what Jay is," he said. "He's my little brother." He laughed, but he put his hand on Jay's shoulder again, the way he had before.

In late August, Ken left for the army. Jay started school right after that. A few guys still wanted to make something out of Jay dancing with Ken. Gordy always threatened to beat up on them, but Jay didn't say too much. He just tried to look those guys in the eye and not hang his head.

Gordy still called him Chief sometimes, but mostly he didn't.

Jay got a letter from Ken in the fall. He was doing okay. Some of the guys hadn't liked having a Japanese-American soldier at basic training, he said. "But I'm showing them what I can do, and they don't worry about it as much as they did at first."

Things were okay for Jay, too. He still hoped he could make it to the major leagues, but there were other things he could do if that didn't work out. Grandpa even said he could take over the drugstore someday, and he was working there a little already. Mom was doing better too, and Hal was becoming almost like part of the family.

Jay still thought about his dad quite often, but he wasn't expecting him to make it home from the war. He had promised his mom that he would remember the good things about him, not all the bad stuff, and that seemed best.

He did think about the war ending someday, and he thought about Ken coming back. Ken hadn't promised that he would make it home, but he'd said he'd try his best. One thing Jay had learned, there were certain promises no one could really make. But he liked to think about being Ken's brother, and he hoped they could be friends all their lives.

Jay and Gordy would always be buddies too, that was for sure. Maybe one of them would even marry Elaine. Mom said she was staying in Delta, and Jay was thinking that was what he wanted to do too.

The main thing was, Jay didn't feel like nothing these days. He felt like a regular guy.